Carmel Bird was born in Tasmania in 1940 and went on from there to continue her studies in France, Spain and California. She has written a novel, *Cherry Ripe*, another collection of short stories, *Births, Deaths and Marriages*, and *Dear Writer* (Virago), a wonderfully illuminating collection of letters to an aspiring writer. She now lives in Melbourne.

Woodpecker Point is a collection of piercing tales, by turns funny, sad, frightening, mysterious, matter-of-fact. Husbands and wives, brothers and sisters, live together but inhabit alarmingly different psychological spaces; familiar images become startling icons; apparently simple stories about childhood become intimate revelations. These are stories that display a unique feeling for the materiality and colour of things and for the perennial mysteries of daily life.

Woodpecker Point

& Other Stories
Carmel Bird

VIRAGO

Published by VIRAGO PRESS Limited 1990
20–23 Mandela Street, Camden Town, London NW1 0HQ

First published as *The Woodpecker Toy Fact and Other Stories* by
McPhee Gribble Publishers, Australia 1987 and in The United States
of America in this selection by New Directions Publishing
Corporation 1988.

Grateful acknowledgment is made to the following Australian publishers
in whose editions these stories first appeared: Allen & Unwin, *Room to
Move* edited by Suzanne Falkiner; Fringe Network, *Soft Lounger* edited
by Antonia Bruns & John Jenkins; Hale & Iremonger, *Strange Attractors*
edited by Damien Broderick; McPhee Gribble/Penguin Books, *The
Woodpecker Toy Fact*; Penguin, *Transgressions* edited by Don
Anderson. *Births, Deaths and Marriages*, the collection from which some
of the stories have been chosen, was privately printed and published. 'In
the Conservatory' is from the book *Room to Move*, edited by Suzanne
Falkiner. Copyright © 1986. Reprinted with permission of the publisher,
Franklin Watts, Inc.

A CIP catalogue record for this title is available from the British Library

Printed in Great Britain by Cox & Wyman Ltd., Reading, Berks

Contents

Boy and Girl

Stephen was six when his sister was born.

Before she was three weeks old, he had made up his mind that he was going to kill her.

His father and his grandmother took him to the hospital to visit his mother. To visit his mother. Since when did he have to *visit* his mother? Since now. Now that Judith was born. Now he had to visit his mother.

The hospital was a dark grey block with gleaming windows. There was ivy and a fountain. It was near the fire station, just where the trams turned round.

They parked the car and walked a long, long way before they came to the hospital gate. Then doors slid open quietly. Stephen and his father and his grandmother went into a great big room full of carpet and armchairs. His mother was not there. They got into a lift with lots of other people. A lady smiled at Stephen. He looked up at her to see that she was nothing like his mother.

His mother was beautiful and pink. She had long silk hair the colour of sand, and her eyes were like the sea. When he rested his head against her breast, he could feel her heart beating. She had lovely little white teeth, silver earrings shaped like shells, and hands which stroked him all over and played songs for him on the piano. He was going to marry her.

They found his mother all alone in a horrible little room where the sun didn't come, and she lay in a high bed under a sheet with blue flowers on it. She looked more beautiful than Stephen remembered. He stood in the doorway and gazed at her.

She was laughing, and his father was kissing her, and his grandmother was crying, and there were vases of flowers all over the place. In his hand, Stephen held a posy of violets. They seemed very little and dull, now that he could see these great leaping stalks of scarlet gladioli, these fat golden roses, naked, miraculously, of thorns.

"Come in, Stephen, come in and say hello to mummy," said his grandmother. "Stephen has been so wonderful, dear, looking after his old grandmother. And his daddy. He has been so looking forward to seeing you, dear, and his little baby sister. He can't wait to see his little baby sister."

Stephen went into the room. He could scarcely feel where his feet were. He was afraid he couldn't walk, he was going to fall over. It seemed to be a very, very long way from the door to the bed. He kept going. The bed was getting closer.

"Come here, Stevie," said his mother. Oh, the beautiful voice. "Come here and sit by me."

He climbed onto the bed and, turning his back on the room, buried his face in his mother's neck. She smelt wonderful. He would stay there forever. He didn't mean to let it happen, but suddenly there were tears all over his face.

This would never do. In his grandmother's world, great big boys of six, she said, simply never cried. He was the big brother now, and must not upset his mother. He must see to it that nothing upset his mother. He must set an example. He must look after his little sister now.

Then a strange thing happened. His grandmother gave him a card, saying, "This is your sister's card. If you hold it up at the nursery window, they will show you your sister. Now isn't that lovely?"

Somehow he stopped crying, and they all went to the nursery

window. His mother held his hand. One of the most glorious things in the world was when his mother took his hand.

They held up the card, and a nurse held up a baby. It was cleverly folded in a blanket, and safely behind a big window. Stephen took very little notice, as he was too happy, holding his mother's warm hand. He did not let go. They all went down in the lift, leaving the baby behind, of course. But then his mother kissed him all over his face, and said she would see him tomorrow. She was going to stay in the hospital.

When Stephen realized that, he felt his heart go grey. A cruel wave of dark water separated him from his mother. And he was cold and still and wrecked. Then he was washed up on the shore of the street outside.

"Let's go to McDonald's," said his father.

They went to McDonald's.

Every day for a week Stephen visited his mother in the hospital. He saw Judith awake, asleep, crying.

"Look, Grannie, look at her waving her hands!"

"She's a dear little baby, and you are a lucky boy."

Then, one day—amazing thing—he was sitting in the garden making a boat from wood and nails when his father drove up, and his mother got out of the car. She was splendid in her long green dress, shimmering. Stephen dropped his hammer and ran to her. Then he stopped.

In one hand she was carrying the baby's basket. In the basket was the baby. Stephen went back to his boat.

He worked hard at the boat all afternoon. When he had finished it, he took it inside and gave it to his mother. She was very pleased, and she hugged him, saying, "That's a beautiful boat, Stevie. You are very clever. When Judith is a little bit older she can sail it in her bath."

"It might sink in the bath," said Stephen.

"We'll see," said his mother, and put it on the bookcase.

Stephen spent a lot of time hammering. He made little houses and tables and rockets and guns.

"It is lovely to see him so contented. And creative," said his grandmother. "Since his sister came, he has been a different boy. Didn't I tell you, dear, that what he needed was a baby brother or sister?"

He spent a lot of time with Judith, too. He rolled her ball to her. She laughed aloud. He took her for rides in the pram. He told her little stories, and even made up songs for her.

> *"I love Judith*
> *She loves me*
> *Oh how happy*
> *We will be*
> *Happy swimming*
> *In the sea."*

She loved the sea. He would gently bury her in sand, and she would shriek with delight. When he made sand castles for her, she liked to smash them down. She ran squealing from the waves as they chased her too, never quite catching her. Then he would grab her by the leg, causing her to fall with a cry of mingled horror and pleasure into the warm shallow creamy foam.

Stephen took Judith out where the water was green. The pebbles rolled under his feet. The sky above was big and bright. There, in the middle of the afternoon, the two little children were caught in the rip and before anybody knew it, they were swept out round the headland. It was never clear whether she had followed her brother into the deep water, or whether he had gone into it to save her. Either way their devotion to each other was quite obvious to everybody. But the knowledge of their love did not warm anybody.

The cruel dark wave of water broke upon the shore.

The beach was empty.

Bye Baby Bunting

Alexander Hunter was forty-five. His hair was dark and wavy, receding. Intelligent blue eyes with a cold edge. He had beautiful smooth pink cheeks, and his teeth, yes his teeth, they were *very* white, with just a few too many pointy ones. These pointy teeth gave his smile an engaging glint, faintly dangerous. Alexander's hands and feet were small, the hands manicured. Always the feet were in shoes sent out from London, custom-made, black or brown. He was of slightly less than average height, slim, with a lovely speaking voice. Usually, he wore grey flannel trousers and a houndstooth jacket. He had a rack of houndstooth jackets in different combinations of colours. They were all of fine soft wool, almost silky to touch, and Alexander was very fond of them. He was a dentist, with rooms on the tenth floor of a luxurious building in Collins Street. In the waiting room, Dr. Hunter kept an enormous tank of tropical fish.

One morning, as he was driving into the city, he glanced across at the driver in the car alongside. There at the wheel sat his ex-wife.

He had not seen her for ten years, but he had never stopped thinking about her. What he always thought was that he wished she

would die. He hoped that one day somebody would look up from
their oysters at one of his dinner parties, and say, casually,

"Oh by the way Alex, did you hear that Gabrielle died last week?"

"How very sad," he would say. "Poor Gabrielle. How did it
happen?"

"Oh," they would say, sipping their wine, "she was practically
eaten alive by some very large dogs on a beach somewhere."

And there she was in the other car, the collar of her enormous
red fox rabbit coat turned up about her ears. She was not dead. She
was not the least bit dead. She was not even sick or old or ugly. Very
alive and cosy in fur, she was pacing him along the freeway in her
filthy white Citroën Goddess.

He lost her at the traffic lights.

He could not catch up with her. Alexander had never really
been able to catch up with Gabrielle. From the beginning, he had
been a man with a butterfly net, chasing her across bright meadows.
As it turned out, she was made from crease-resistant material, un-
crushable. He thought he had caught her. Yes it looked as if he had
caught his butterfly. After the wedding, he put her in a big gabled
house in Kew, and gave her a handful of credit cards.

He told her she was free to decorate the house as she wished.
One day he came home to discover scarlet silk curtains hung with
silver bells across the centre of the hall. Then he went upstairs to the
bedroom where Gabrielle was painting a mural on the ceiling. It was
a picture of the sky, moving from pink and blue clouds with butterflies on one side, to navy blue night, full of golden stars, on the
other.

Alexander was speechless with astonishment.

He went to the telephone and called an interior decorator. It
was the only sensible thing to do. Next he called the airline and
booked Gabrielle on a flight to Perth. She could stay with her sister
for a while.

"I'll get the house done for you, darling pet. It's such a big job.
You go and have a good time in Perth. Don't you worry about a
thing."

When Gabrielle came back from Perth, the house was carpet-

ed in beige. The walls were pale apricot or soft cinnamon. There
were cream silk drapes and parchment lamps. The dining room was
papered in pale grey, embossed with shadows of moths. A large
stuffed trout stared out from a glass case on the wall. The curtains
were grey velvet. There were antiques and indoor plants, puffy pale
sofas, discreet slivers of watery stained glass. In the hall, Alexander
kept an enormous tank of tropical fish.

"This must have cost a fortune, Alex," said Gabrielle.

"Oh yes, it did. I'm glad you like it."

And they had dinner parties. White linen, silver, white china,
the finest glass. Alexander selected the wines from his cellar. He had
been busily buying wines for years, and his cellar was the envy of
everybody. Caterers did the food which Alexander chose.
Everybody agreed that it was delicious. Gabrielle was a charming
hostess. And she did the flowers.

"She glows, she scintillates. Alexander is so lucky. They are so
happy. Did you see the flowers. She's a genius with flowers. Grows
them all herself too. The poinsettias were extraordinary, didn't you
think? She seems very fond of red flowers. There are always red
flowers."

Behind the house there was a long garden. Alexander walked
in the garden on Sunday afternoons with a cigar. A glass of brandy
in one hand. There would be other dentists with cigars and brandy
walking with him. Sometimes an obstetrician or the conductor of an
orchestra. Their wives were in the drawing room with Gabrielle, sipping coffee and Tia Maria. They ate chocolates and smoked black
Sobranies. They talked about recipes and dressmakers and their last
trip to New York. Some of them had babies, and they talked about
them.

"I think I'd like to go to Italy," said Gabrielle.

"Oh so would I," said one of the wives. "Let's learn Italian."

And so they did. On Wednesdays and Fridays, the wives went
to Italian classes. Some of them became quite fluent. One had an
affair with the tutor, but he went back to Italy and nothing came of
it. It was just a ripple which briefly disturbed the even surface of
their lives. Then they took up tapestry, and the tutor was a grand-

mother with twinkling eyes and a wealth of ideas on how to decorate cushions.

Gabrielle tired of the tapestry, and went back to her garden. Sweet violets and lavender. She loved to be surrounded by green, to smell the earth. To see the buds of her red roses open. Her roses rambled out of control.

In a dark corner, water trickled from a fountain, hidden by vines. A secret place where Gabrielle went to think or read or draw. She loved to draw. And paint. Birds, butterflies, flowers, monsters, fairies. Gabrielle sat in her cool green grotto by the fountain, drawing fairies.

Then she decided to play the flute. Alexander was pleased. He rather liked the flute. He found her a teacher, and came home one evening with a flute and a stack of music and manuscript books.

Gabrielle was becoming so accomplished, Alexander thought. Civilised. Perhaps she was almost ready for the responsibilities of motherhood.

Here was the problem. In most ways, Alexander seemed to have Gabrielle under control but he was actually rather afraid of her. She was complicated, dramatic, demanding, wild, incomprehensible. So unlike Debbie, his little nurse to whom he frequently made quick lunchtime love in the second surgery. With Debbie it was business. Nice. Over and done with. Crazy Gabrielle wanted to make it a way of life. Well, life was about much more than sex, he tried to tell her. There was money to be made, people to entertain, concerts to go to, conferences to attend.

"Yes, I see," Gabrielle would say, and disappear into the garden to draw fairies or play the flute. Was that all she did in the garden? Perhaps when he was busy filling teeth and making money, she met a lover in the grotto. Perhaps.

Alexander chose not to dwell on that. The question that preoccupied him was—would he be able to give Gabrielle a child. That was the real question, deep down. On the surface, he phrased it differently. He said—will Gabrielle be able to give me a child. Another question which he did not encounter except in dreams was—did he really want a child. But that was *quite* a different matter.

He was a successful dentist with a beautiful home, a Jaguar, and a Mercedes. He was having a pool built by the side of the house. His wife was a wonderful hostess. The next thing he needed was a son.

One night, he and Gabrielle were invited out to dinner. Alexander, wooing and taming her, had bought her flowers and perfume. In the window of an antique shop, in a red velvet case, he saw a magnificent old silver flute. Then he went down to the Windsor to have a drink with some visiting professors. He stayed, as he always did, longer than he had meant.

By the time he got home to pick up Gabrielle they were already an hour late for dinner.

"I have been sitting here ringing around trying to find you. I have rung Susan. She is going ahead with dinner now. They're not going to wait for us. I can't stand being caught up with you in this kind of rudeness, Alex."

"Oh, they'll understand. Don't get excited. Look, I've bought something for you."

He took from behind his back the flowers, the perfume, and the flute.

Gabrielle had turned her back. She was putting on her red fox rabbit coat.

"What?" she looked around.

"I've brought my little Gabrielle a wonderful silver flute. See."

She snatched the flowers and hurled them across the room so that salmon pink and cochineal spears of gladioli littered the carpet, the bed.

"You stupid bloody fool!" she yelled. "If you can't do a simple decent thing like getting to Susan's on time, who wants your flowers and your fucking flute! I don't want your flute. The price is too high. Far too high. Take your flute and go away. Go away!"

She went to Susan's alone. It was the first time people had seen her at dinner without Alex.

"He had to go away suddenly," she explained.

She was a brilliant success at dinner.

The flute stayed in a cupboard. Alex had it insured. The incident was over. Life went on with conferences and dinner parties and gardening. What did Gabrielle do in the garden?

They did not have a baby.

Gabrielle finally left Alexander and went off with an American opera singer called Charles.

It happened like this.

One night in the grey mothy dining room, under the eye of the dead fish, Charles and some other singers from the opera sat at dinner. Charles was next to Gabrielle. She thought he was lovely. They talked about music until they came to flutes.

"In New York," said Charles, "I have a very old flute. Silver. One day I'm going to take it up seriously."

"An old silver flute," said Gabrielle. Alexander glared at her. "I have an old silver flute in the cupboard. Just excuse me a moment everybody. Please." And she was gone. Alex stared after her for a moment in disbelief at her carelessness of his feelings. Then he recovered. She came back with the flute in its red velvet box and handed it to Charles. He admired it. Everybody admired it.

"Yes," said Alex, "it's quite a valuable antique."

Charles put it to his lips and played a simple tune.

"You ought to learn to play the flute. Take lessons," said Alex. The guests were surprised by the acidity of his tone.

"Give it to me now. I am going to put it away. As I said, it's a valuable antique."

"No Alex," said Gabrielle quietly. "It is my flute, and I would like Charles to play it."

"When he learns to play," said Alex.

The grey room was very quiet.

Gabrielle took the flute from Charles. She put it in its case. Then she stood up and said,

"Charles, could I speak to you for a moment. Do excuse us, won't you everybody. Help yourselves to sweets. Please do."

Gabrielle and Charles left the room. They left the house. And they never came back.

It was a tremendous scandal. Excited dentists and their wives discussed it at dinner, over the telephone, in bars, at sewing afternoons, coffee mornings. Poor Alex was distraught. They comforted him.

There was a divorce. Gabrielle went to New York. Alex pulled himself together and went on with his life. One day he would get another wife, but in the meantime he never had any trouble finding beautiful women to be hostesses at his dinner table, partners at the theatre.

When he saw Gabrielle in the car, it was a shock. He contained his rage for a week, going about his life as usual, perhaps getting a little more drunk in the evenings.

On Sunday, he took the Jaguar and drove into the country. His two Jack Russells, great little hunting dogs, went with him. They all had a fine time in the open air, and Alexander shot fourteen rabbits and a fox.

He was an excellent shot.

Brother Gregory

"Take your hand off my knee!" cried the duchess.

"Well, somebody had better have a hand on the duchess's knee, and he had better mean business."

My father was a writer. He earned his living as a court reporter, but he claimed that his real work was on the great Australian novel. He never wrote it. Words, however, were his trade, and when I was about twelve, he looked at some of my stories. He said that I was "over-promising" things. I was leading the reader up the garden path. I was not delivering the goods.

"If you take them up the garden path, Margery, there has to be at least an escaped lunatic in the woodshed. If not a homicidal maniac."

But at other times he would say:

"Write about what you *know*, Margery, only about what you *know*."

Well, I couldn't very well write about a homicidal maniac, could I? I had never met one, I argued.

"Don't worry, don't worry about it at all," said my father. "We are all homicidal maniacs here."

He meant that, actually. He had spent so many years in court that he believed anybody to be capable of anything, given the circumstances. "Original sin," he would say, "I'm a great believer in original sin. And sometimes, you know, baptism doesn't take. And furthermore, there are so many un-baptised sinners running around loose."

Many of his sayings, such as "We are all homicidal maniacs here," became family jokes. When Jehovah's Witnesses or Mormons came to the door to be turned away with "We are all Catholics here," somebody would yell down the hall: "No we're not! We're all homicidal maniacs!" And everyone would laugh as at the world's funniest joke. Another one of these sayings was the one about the hand on the duchess's knee.

So when Brother Gregory from the novitiate, where our own brother Nicholas was a student, put his hand on my sister's knee, she should have been prepared. But she wasn't. I was watching when he did it, and I wasn't prepared either. Father's jokes were not always useful as a preparation for life.

I had never really followed up the story about the duchess, and Dympna, my sister, did not say or scream anything. She just sat very still and stared straight ahead.

You are wondering how all this came about.

When Nicholas went into the novitiate, Brother Gregory was appointed as his sort of special guardian "within the walls" as we used to say. We, that is Dympna and I, thought from the start that he was a horrible looking creature for a guardian. He was fat and pink with sandy bristles running in ripples on his freckled neck. He had bulbous blue eyes with thick glasses, and dreadful big square feet. Square red hands hung from his fat black sleeves. Father said he was a perfect example of a particular Irish type. "You see," he said, "there's the black Irish, the white Irish, and what we have here, this Brother Gregory, is the square Irish. Yes, in Ireland, square is a colour. Very useful in a brawl. If he's on your side, of course. Keep him on your side and you'll come to no harm."

He smelt of stale tobacco.

On Thursday nights, Brother Gregory often came to dinner. Mother went quite silly over him, actually. She would simper and twitter and serve his favourite wing rib with tomato pie. She was always inclined to pander to members of the clergy. In this case, we thought she was definitely casting pearls before swine.

Brother Gregory would report to her on Nicholas's progress. Then he would drink Father's port and smoke a cigar, sucking loudly and letting the ash fall on his lapels and onto the carpet as well. This infuriated Dympna as she was responsible for keeping the dining room carpet clean. Father was seldom present at these dinners, but would sometimes turn up for the port.

"A court reporter," he would say, "is a very busy fellow, and finds it necessary to pursue his profession in the company of his colleagues and other criminals in the back bar of any one of fifty distinguished pubs. So I cannot always join you people for dinner. But a port now. Brother, a port?"

"Joseph," Mother would say, smiling indulgently, "you are nothing but a professional drinker."

"You're right, Alice. I am that, and proud of it. It's a fine living. Look at us now—beautiful roof of slates over our heads, decorated with griffins to ward off the evil spirits. We have wing rib and tomato in our stomachs. Children, dozens of them, all at the very best schools. Don't worry about the ash at all, Brother Gregory. Dympna will see to it."

Brother Gregory had been unaware of the ash.

He did not like Father. He sensed that Father did not welcome him, but of course he knew he had a right to be there. There was nothing really personal in Father's attitude to him. Father found the whole human race endearing in its vanity. Folly amused him; wickedness fascinated him. He was altogether too witty and intelligent for old Brother Gregory of the square Irish.

We all had to control our laughter, as we knew that Father was saying to us that Brother Gregory was a pure example of the square.

"I wouldn't disagree with you on that now, Mr. O'Connor," answered Brother Gregory. Was he implying that he would disagree with Father on a lot of other things? I think he was. And I believe that Father thought so too. He went on:

"Yes. Black Irish, I said, the moment I set eyes on her. And I named her after the Irish princess who was her father's favourite, you know. Furthermore, she's the patron saint of the insane. Did you know that Brother? I expect you did. Yes, I thought it wouldn't be a bad idea to have the patron of the insane smile on the home. It has worked well, as you can see. We're all mad. Was it the Cheshire Cat who said, 'I'm mad. You're mad?' But no, Brother Gregory, you're not mad. I exclude Brother Gregory. He is quite, quite sane!"

"We are all homicidal maniacs here," said Dympna.

Brother Gregory blinked at her with his popping blue eyes. He looked uncomfortable. Mother and I had gone to do the washing up by this time, but we could hear the conversation from the kitchen. All she said was,

"Margery, your father's a terrible tease sometimes. Poor Brother Gregory."

It was cruel of father to do that to Brother Gregory, but he found it irresistible. And he did it every time they met, somehow or other. Brother Gregory knew that something had happened to him, that he had been subtly diminished. But he didn't quite know how.

I was puzzled that this foolish fat man with little splashes of old dinners on his jacket should be Nicholas's guardian "within the walls". Father made a fool of him; mother flirted a little with him. What were we to make of him? What did Nicholas think of him? We never really knew. However, our little brother summed it all up when he said,

"He stinks, and I hate him."

It was 1956. Dympna was seventeen, I was fifteen, and our sister, Pauline, was getting married. Brother Gregory offered to chauffeur some of the family home from the reception. It was Dympna and I who went with him.

She sat in the front of the car, and I sat in the back. We had been the bridesmaids, in frivolous puffs of blue organdie. We were about half-way home when I saw Brother Gregory's square red hand move across and land heavily on Dympna's skirt. It was an unceremonious and slightly drunken action. Dympna went very still and quiet. I stared. It was as if some horrible, paralysing spider had landed on us both. The car seemed to be going very, very slowly, in perfect silence. Outside, the world was sliding darkly by. Frozen, helpless, bewildered, we sat there as the hand began to fiddle with the frilly skirt, and Brother Gregory felt my stare. He turned his head to catch my gaze and then turned away.

Knowledge came to me suddenly as I sat there in the back of the gliding Chevrolet. I knew with a harsh clarity that Brother Gregory hated us. He hated Dympna and me, hated Pauline's wedding, but most of all I knew that he hated Father. Father was so vital. Brother Gregory hated life. And I realised that he was destructive.

By the time we reached the house the hand had moved very little. The lights downstairs were all on; the door wide open. No-one spoke in the car. Dympna and I opened the doors in unison and walked slowly, in dignified silence, towards the house. I retain a stark memory of a large green glass vase full of irises on the hall table. Their stems through the glass. Criss cross of green stems through green glass under water. From our dresses, confetti fell onto the carpet.

Brother Gregory and his car had gone into the night.

We told nobody about our ride home. Brother Gregory never came to dinner again, and I have never seen him since. It was only a few weeks after Pauline's wedding that Nicholas came out of the novitiate. Naturally, the two events are connected in my mind, although they may not be related.

Nicholas said that he had been told he was unsuited to the order. The brothers had been concerned that he would "miss the joys of family life," he said.

"Oh yes, you would," said Father. "I'm sure you would that." The joys of family life became a family joke.

The Balloon Lady

Grand-mère was an enormous navy blue person, navy blue from her velvet hat to her sensible, elegant lace-ups. Large navy tear drops swung from her ears. On her stuffed bosom there sat a dull dove. She was very tall and, I think, looking back on it now, that she must have been modelling herself on Queen Mary, with a touch of General de Gaulle. Her name was Marie-Louise, and I am named for her. She was an anglophile and smelt of Devon Violets. She always had oval slivers of amber Pears' soap in her bathroom. She read Agatha Christie and P.G. Wodehouse in the original English, much to the astonishment of my mother who came from a less educated family than papa.

So it was no doubt grand-mère who saw to it that I had a good English au pair. Rosemary came to us when I was a baby and she was still there when Yvette was born, three years later. She stayed until I was six, and that is a very long time for an au pair.

She was little and pretty. "Rosemary—dew of the sea—" grand-mère would say. She had long dark curls, and slightly oriental eyes, and grand-mère would go on to declaim about the fact that Rosemary was a true English rose—something which, years later, I could never quite tie in with the eyes. I thought she was rather like a little white gipsy. But of course grand-mère was determined that Rosemary would be an English "type". So she was.

Grand-mère and grand-père lived in Ville d'Avray which is just outside Paris. They had one of those two-storey houses with green shutters that you see in travel posters. Very square and formal, with a faint apricot blush to the stone. In front there were two squares of lawn with a mulberry tree in the middle of one, and an apple tree in the other. At the back was a long garden with fruit trees at the bottom. Between the house and the trees, grand-père grew vegetables. He was a little thin man with a neat white moustache and wire spectacles which I admired. I remember that his favourite delicacy was Port Salut. He used to be a sailor and talked a lot about the sea. He used to play a little Basque bagpipe which he called by its German name "dudelsack". On a still, hot night at sea, long ago, he said, a mermaid rose up from the water to listen. Mermaids, he told me, are very fond of music, and very partial indeed to the dudelsack. Just once he saw her, and never again. But of course he never forgot her. She had skin like living snow, he said.

"Did she sing, grand-père? Did she sing to the music?"

"She sang, she sang. Oh yes, she sang a Basque lullaby. And then she disappeared."

"And you never saw her again."

"And I never saw her again."

"You searched the seven seas for her."

"I searched the seven seas for my mermaid, yes."

"Playing the dudelsack?" Then I would scream with laughter and grand-père would pretend he was going to strike me with his stick because he was insulted.

Over and over again I would ask him to tell me the story about his mermaid. It was like a dead bell inside me when he said: "And I never saw her again."

Sometimes in the summer, under the trees in the evening, he would play little dance tunes on his pipes. Rosemary sang, and I would dance, barefoot in the grass. Then grand-mère would appear at the top of the garden like a navy monolith saying, "Bed time Marie-Louise!" and the spell was broken.

I seem to have spent a good deal of time at Ville d'Avray. I think it was partly because grand-mère wanted to talk to Rosemary about London and the Queen and the Sussex downs. Rosemary was actually more interested in Paris and clothes and makeup. But she would humour grand-mère and give her English newspapers and sweets from Callard and Bowser. I think she used to make up the stuff about the Queen. I like to think so, as it is a little triumph over grand-mère who was so righteous and powerful and had no sense of humour.

A lot of my life was also spent in Paris. We lived in the sixteenth, in a vast old apartment. On the ground floor, in a smelly little glass box, rather like a railway carriage, was the concierge. There was another powerful woman. She knew everything about everybody, spending much of her time sitting on a chair in the street, talking, talking, talking to other concierges. And to everyone else as well. She wore greasy black and grey clothes, many of them knitted. They wound about her like a cocoon, and her face was a walnut with whiskers. She was a kind friend but a deadly enemy. I concentrated on keeping her as a friend, and from a very early age I practised a dazzling smile with which I fed her at least four times a day. She always gave Rosemary a long cold look, and pretended not to understand her French.

Our life in Paris was ordered, formal. There were regular times for meals and baths and sleeps. Every day at two we went to the Parc Monceau with Rosemary. I remember walking there, holding the side of the great big English pram in which Rosemary pushed Yvette. The pram lived under the stairs, next to the concierge, along with the bicycles and other prams from all the other apartments. Sometimes Rosemary needed help to get it out, as the wheels became entangled. The concierge would stare blankly at her as she explained the problem. I wanted to bite the concierge on the nose. When we crossed the road to go to the park, I could feel the panic in Rosemary's tightening hand. She was very afraid of the traffic.

At last we would reach the pavement outside the park, with a great sigh, and sometimes a laugh. There, by the gate, on an iron

chair, sat the balloon lady. She was fat and kept the money jingling
in a leather apron. Her feet bulged out of tartan slippers, very dirty.

She had a fat face, teeth like a rat, and a few white whiskers.
She sucked air in through her teeth, and smelt of cake. Above her,
in a lumpy rainbow cloud, shivered the balloons.
Pink-lemon-scarlet-and-green.

"Which one would you like, Marie-Louise?"

"All of them!"

That was the truth. I wanted all the balloons, and the balloon
lady as well. What a glorious, what a splendid thing that would be.
To march first around the park and then across the road and up the
street to the apartment, holding the balloon lady by one hand, and
ALL THE BALLOONS in the other! We would sail past the
astounded and shrivelling concierge, who might even faint or die
from shock, and up the stairs. Inside the apartment we would tie the
balloons to the hallstand. There they would fill the hall with globes
of glowing colour. We would leave the balloons there to surprise all
who entered, and proceed with our balloon lady to the salon where
we would all take a goûter of very special things. There would be
pain-chocolat and delicious rissoles made by maman from horse-
meat rolled in sugar. And champagne. I always used to think that
the only thing to drink when the balloon lady came to tea would be
champagne. In fine pink glasses. Grand-père would be there, and he
would play the Basque cradle song. Rosemary would sing; I would
dance. Yvette, I think, had been put to bed. I saw Rosemary then as
the re-incarnation of the lost mermaid, chaplets of water dripping
from her hair.

It was winter when grand-père suddenly appeared in the Parc
Monceau. Yvette was rolling a red rubber ball around the gravel,
and I, in my mittens and boots, was climbing the ladder, when out
of nowhere, there he was. He looked smaller and thinner and more
grey and white than I remembered. He was just a little shadow of
an old sea captain, buttoned neatly into his navy blue overcoat,
leaning a little on his stick, and blowing mushrooms of steam into
the air. He sat on the seat next to Rosemary. Their faces were serious and their heads were bowed, very close together. It seemed to

me that perhaps grand-mère was ill, or, dare I think it, dead. But grand-père and Rosemary said nothing to me.

Then we were all walking to the gate. Yvette carrying the red ball, carefully like a bright treasure. Past the fountain choked with leaves.

"There she is, grand-père, the balloon lady!" I ran towards her because I knew grand-père would buy us balloons. She smiled with her rat teeth which I liked so much, and I got a good whiff of cake. Grand-père gave her the money in his grey woollen glove. My balloon was pink, Yvette's was blue, and grand-père bought a green one for Rosemary. I thought that was funny, and I started to laugh.

"Rosemary doesn't get a balloon! She never gets a balloon."

But grand-père didn't answer. In spite of the balloons, the grim atmosphere stayed. He walked with us to the front door. The concierge nodded. Then grand-père disappeared into the winter afternoon. Gone.

The next morning there was no Rosemary. I ran from room to room calling to her. Overnight all trace of her was removed, except for a tin of barley sugars and the green balloon.

I heard papa say to maman:
"He's a silly old idiot, of course, but I really don't see why our lives should be disrupted by his indiscretions. Mother is an interfering old bag of wind. And ridiculous, whatsmore. She's ridiculous and he's a fool! Oh blast them."

All he said to me was:
"Rosemary had to return to England suddenly. She will not be coming back." I cried for days.

The green balloon burst.

When it became clear that Rosemary really wasn't coming back, and that she wasn't going to write me a letter, I began to blame the balloon lady. I didn't like her teeth or her smell any more, and I never really wanted a balloon. The hall would never be filled with rainbow bubbles, and the concierge would never fall down dead at the sight of me.

The next summer I went to school.

Mother of the Bride

"**W**hen I grow up," said Emily, "I'm going to be a man." That was in 1926 when Emily was five. It was Christmas, and Emily and her brothers, her father and mother, her uncles, aunts, grannies, grandpas, and all her cousins were sitting around the Christmas tree in the hall. The girls were given pink dolls in white dresses, and the boys were given bows and arrows. Emily, in yellow georgette, with a puff of golden ringlets, looked with envy at those bows and arrows, and said very loudly, "When I grow up, I'm going to be a man."

Everyone laughed and then they all went into the dining room for goose and pudding, burning on a dish.

Emily was strong and adventurous. She won prizes for riding and swimming, and also for music and mathematics. At the university she studied law. She met Dennis who was also studying law, and after a year or so they became engaged.

It was then that Emily began to collect in earnest the china and silver and linens for her future home. Her thoughts from then on were all of the charming nest she would furnish with Dennis. People were astonished.

"But Emily," they said, "this is not like you, all this talk of Waterford crystal and balloon-back chairs!"

Her uncles smiled benignly; her aunts beamed with delight and gave her parties.

"Then this must be the real me," said Emily with a laugh. "I never really cared for law. Dennis will be the lawyer for us all."

A little corner of her spirit twisted and squirmed when Emily said that. But she quieted it and went on hemming table mats.

She began to have what she called her "Sleeping Beauty Dreams". They were the most peculiar dreams that Emily could have imagined. Fancy dreaming that you were asleep and dreaming. She was in some kind of old grey castle which was buried in blackberry bushes. She knew that from the air it looked like a solid ball of blackberries. Inside she lay on a vast pink bed in a pink, pink room, with her hands crossed on her breast. Long, long golden hair fanned across the pillow. She dreamt. Of what did she dream? That was the tantalizing part. Emily never knew what she was dreaming about in her dream. And in the dream, she never woke up. When, in reality, she did wake up, she always felt floaty and dreamy. It was a rather nice feeling, Emily thought.

In white lace, she married Dennis. It was all very simple because of the war. They lived in a sweet little flat until the first baby was born. Then they bought a great big house with bay windows and an enormous garden. Dennis was doing very well in the city. They had a second daughter and when the two little girls went to school Emily went on committees with her friends and raised hundreds and hundreds of pounds for those less fortunate than she.

When the time came for the elder daughter, Caroline, to be married, Emily became the mother of the bride.

Forgotten long ago was the declaration of her wish to own a bow and arrow and be a man. When Emily grew up she finally became the mother of the bride.

It was such a busy and exciting time for Emily. She made plans and lists and telephone calls. She bullied and cajoled and manipulated. She wrote cheques. Emily was a perfectionist. She was an organiser. Her years of work on committees had trained her for this glorious position of mother of the bride.

She controlled Caroline's wedding from the quality of the

paper for the invitations to the signing of the lease on the flat. One of the bridesmaids complained about the dresses.

"Why do we have to wear this pus-coloured hailspot muslin?"

"Wheat, dear, the colour is wheat," said Emily smoothly. They wore the hailspot muslin.

Caroline carried a sheaf of wheat mixed with cornflowers, daisies, and scarlet poppies.

"So unusual, Emily," said her friends. "But you always were original, and what a beautiful setting."

Emily, in honey-coloured silk, stood in the sunlight of her garden, which was one of her finest creations. She was an expert on fertilisers and pesticides. No snail could lurk for long but Emily would track it down. No thrip would dare to settle on the petals of her roses. Sandstone steps led from one part of the garden to another. Smooth lawns, dark conifers, and flower beds which changed with the seasons. For the wedding, Emily had planted gold and white.

Some child vomited in the fish pond.

"Remember that Christmas, Em," said one of her brothers, "when the boys got bows and arrows, and you wanted one badly, and you said you were going to be a man when you grew up?"

"Did I? How very awkward for everybody!"

"Well, they just laughed. And when all's said and done, it was very funny."

"And you remembered."

"Yes, I've always remembered that. It stuck, somehow. Not very prophetic. It's a grand wedding, Em. You look young enough to be the bride yourself."

Then he was gone, chatting in his easy manner to everyone. He didn't seem to have to bully people as she did. Emily envied that skill of his. She envied also, all over again, the bows and arrows of those years ago. How long? Forty-five years.

The feeling of Christmas day came back to her. And with it the silly pink dolls in their frilly dresses with their fat arms. She saw the bows, powerful with their dangerous arrows. A terrible sadness engulfed her for a moment.

It was just then that one of the bees that were murmuring in the flowers stung Emily on the hand. She was particularly sensitive to bees, and her arm began to swell. A guest who was a doctor gave her an injection.

"He probably saved my life. I blew up like a balloon. And the agony!"

She lay in the dark in her pink bedroom. She dreamt her Sleeping Beauty Dream, but this time, when she woke up she was crying. She was remembering the bow and arrow, and the tears came spilling out of her. She gulped and sobbed.

A cloud moved through the summer sky. The lightning, the thunder, the rain came and scattered the party in the garden.

The Woodpecker Toy Fact

My mother was a magger.*

A paling fence divided our garden from the garden next-door, and over the back fence lived Mrs Back-Fence. My mother and Mrs Back-Fence might have been posing for a cartoonist as they stood on either side of the fence, magging. Behind each woman was a rotary clothes-line. We had striped tea-towels, white sheets, woollen singlets, pink pants, and knitted socks all hanging from dolly pegs. Some things were patched and darned, the mending being more obvious when the clothes were wet. It was unsafe to hang anything damaged but unmended on the line, for this would be noted by other maggers as a sign of degeneration in the family. And once, when a torn, unmended nightdress had got through the washing and as far as the line, our rabbit attacked it and shredded it so that it had to be thrown out. My mother and Mrs Back-Fence had floral aprons, and often their hair was set with metal butterfly wavers, covered by a chiffon scarf knotted at the front. They did not wear fluffy slippers. Instead they nearly always wore rather thick stockings and brown lace-up shoes, like nurses.

---

*The magpie is the scandalmonger of the woods. The verb 'to mag' meaning 'to gossip' derives from magpie.

Over the back fence, these maggers passed hot scones wrapped in tea-towels, cups of sugar, bowls of stewed plums, and a continuous ribbon of talk. They sifted through the details of everything they heard and saw and thought, and arranged them into art. Children under the age of ten, considered to lack the ability to understand the narrative, were allowed to listen, provided they were still and quiet. (Today, magging usually takes place on the telephone, I think, and so a child listener becomes restless because there is only one side to the conversation.) The Crusaders took from the Arabian desert the seeds of the wild flowers which later became the glory of English gardens. The maggers scoured the lives of their relations and neighbours, and sometimes the lives of famous people, to shake out the seeds from which would grow undulating plains of exotic grasses and flowers giving colour and perfume.

One of the most hypnotic habits of the maggers was the constant use of possessive pronouns and parentheses. They constructed sentences which could go on all day in dizzy convolutions as one relative clause after another was added.

"Edna and Joe (his brother was Colin who married Betty Trethewey who later divorced him which was when he had his breakdown over the Kelly girl so that it was no wonder the business went down-hill) were having their twenty-fifth anniversary which was just before Easter which was early that year, and Pam (she's the daughter, you realize) was there with her fiancé who was Bruce French (his father had the hardware next to the Royal Park) when it turned out that Joe was electrocuted in the cellar which was where he kept the wine (they drank a terrible lot of wine in those days) and it wasn't long after that that Edna turned round and married Bruce, and Pam went and lived next-door to them (this was fifteen years ago now) and she hasn't spoken to them since which is very hard on the daughter, Susan, who doesn't even know that Bruce is her father, not that Bruce can be certain himself really, but of course Edna knows and she has never forgiven Pam for not telling her she was going to have Susan when she was engaged to Bruce."

As a child I never saw any Marx Brothers films. When I *did* see them, I was surprised to hear Groucho Marx using my mother's phrases. Trapped in her language, like fish in a net, were snatches and snippets from the Marx Brothers' scripts. Inserted into the magging of two women in a Tasmanian coastal town of the 1940s, the expressions of Groucho Marx had a curious lifelessness, and their meaning was elusive. But I, as a child, accepted the words at face-value, in faith, expecting to have their meaning revealed in good time. It took many years for things to fall into place. Perhaps the child who called his bear Gladly after Gladly the cross-eyed bear is an apocryphal child, but the story has a nice ring of truth. Harold be thy name. I applied the same unblinking acceptance to the name of the local toy shop. The end of the sign had fallen off, and so it was called "The Woodpecker Toy Fact". I even accepted the name of the toymaker as an ordinary name, and now I don't know whether it was his real name or not. He was called Jack Frost. At Christmas, he used to make wooden peepshows of the crib. You closed one eye and looked through the hole in the box. Inside, in an unearthly light were first the shepherds, then the animals, and further back, the baby like a sugar mouse in his mother's arms. The angels were in the far distance, wings sharp like the wings of swallows. And Jack Frost carved our rocking-horse. Even the name of the horse, Dapple Grey, I failed to see as descriptive, and thought of as Christian name and surname. I must have existed in a blurry blue mist where I waited for the words to acquire meaning. Something which I always connected with the verb "to mag" was some stuff called "Milk of Mag". This was a thick, white, slightly aniseed, shudderingly horrible laxative medicine, the "Mag" being short for magnesia.

I tried to join in some magging once. I made the mistake of thinking that if I introduced some fabulous fact, I would be included in the discussion. So I said that Jack Frost had told me he had made the original statue of the Infant Jesus of Prague. Nobody took any notice of me at all. Or so I thought. But after a while I realised that terribly silly lies were being referred to as woodpecker toy facts.

"And then she tried to tell me the baby was premature. A woodpecker toy fact if ever I heard one. It is no mystery to me that he weighed nine and a half pounds. Nine and a half pounds! I ask you."

There was a special quality to a toy fact. There was a desperation—either to attract or to deflect attention. And a toy fact only became a toy fact after it had passed through the special sifting process of the maggers, and had received from them a blessing.

So I had generated a term which had drifted into the net of the maggers. Little did I know (as a magger would say) that the spirit of my words was being given the same weight as that accorded the words of Groucho Marx.

Over the years, the concept of the woodpecker toy fact has become very important and dear to me. I have lived here in Woodpecker Point on the northwest coast of Tasmania all my life. My parents have died and my sisters have all married and left the island. I live alone in the house with the rotary clothes-line and the paling fence. Mrs Back-Fence is in a nursing home in Burnie, and I have never seen the wife of the Turkish man who now lives in the house. They have a baby daughter who sings Baa-baa-black-sheep sadly and endlessly in the garden. It is a very boring and irritating song, after a while. Jack Frost has disappeared. One of my nephews took Dapple Grey to the beach and left him there and he was washed out to sea. As these and many other things have changed, so the idea of the toy fact has changed and developed. The quest for the toy fact has gradually come to dominate my life.

Once when I was at the beach, years before the toy fact was named, I captured a star fish in my tin bucket. The tide was out, and there was a cold breeze coming in across the shiny wet sand. I was sitting on the pebbles which were shaped like eggs, and smooth, and all different kinds of white. I had the bucket between my legs so that I could stare down into it at the star fish, and I was given the ability to understand the shape of everything. The moment passed, and yet it has never left me. Five minutes later, the sky went darker, and a red-haired girl in a green dress came up behind me and grabbed the bucket. She ran off across the pebbles with the star fish. My second oldest sister chased the girl, and the girl defended herself with the spike of a beach umbrella. She drove the spike into my sister's lip, ran off with the bucket, and disappeared.

I think my quest began with the star fish. Perhaps if that girl had not stolen it when she did, had not injured my sister as she did, I might never have undertaken the quest. Then, when the toy fact was named and its nature defined in a rudimentary way, I sensed that there was a system of knowing things which could, if handled in the right way, lead to an understanding, the idea of which dazzled me. The simplicity and complexity of the star fish, punctuated in time by my sister's blood, and coupled with the glorious lie (which might not have been a lie) about Jack Frost and the Infant of Prague, suggested to me that if I assembled facts in a special way every minute of every day for years and years and years, I would eventually see something more beautiful and more wonderful than anything I could have imagined. It was as though I had a golden thread which I wove to make a net in which I caught the toy facts, trapping them, bright birds in flight, planets in amber. I have collected and assembled the toy facts in my brain, and I am still uncertain as to whether I will ultimately discover *The Toy Fact*, and so complete the pattern, or whether, by placing the final *Fact* I will produce *The Toy Fact*. The quest itself is, however, absorbing, and has, as I said, come to dominate my life.

It is not only a matter of discovering things, but of manufacturing from those things the toy facts in all their fullness and beauty. I sometimes think my golden net of facts is like a fabulous story I am writing in my head. Once when I was studying poetry at school, I used to think that everything was a metaphor, and said "metaphor" in answer to every question.

"If we took a slice off the top of her head," said the teacher, and I thought she was going to pay me a compliment, "we would find that the only thing in there was a metaphor." She meant to be insulting, but had stumbled on the beautiful truth. It was that remark of hers that set me on my final course. From then on, I did not have to pass any exams or do anything much at all. I have spent my time since that day listening to people, reading encyclopaedias, browsing in the library, sitting on the beach, and generally pursuing one toy fact after another. I cared for my parents when they were ill, and I have worked in the Morning Glory cake shop for the past ten years.

One day, I am going to know everything about everything. I will know what makes a Cox's Orange Pippin different from a Granny Smith. I will know what it is that stops hydrangeas from having any scent. I will see the pyramids being built and survive the Hundred Years' War. I will understand the nature of fire, and know the depth to which the longest tree-root goes down in the earth. I will know what sorrow is made from, what constitutes joy. I will have conversations with the sage of Zurich, afternoon tea with Chagall in his garden, speak to Polycrates the King before his crucifixion in Magnesia. There are bound to be times when I can think in Chinese.

Meanwhile, I live here in Woodpecker Point, not far from the ruins of the park where the deer and the peacocks used to roam. I prune the roses and the fruit trees and I talk to my finches.

I have a large collection of feathers, and am making a study of their colours. I am particularly interested at present in the iridescent colours which ripple and change on the necks of pigeons. They are formed when the light is refracted from the surfaces of the tiny scales which make up the feathers. I suppose some colours of reptiles and butterflies work on the same principle. I have spent a lot of time with butterflies, and can here, quite naturally, in the course, as it were, of the conversation, mention a very high-class toy fact. This is the fact that the Cabbage White Butterfly arrived in Tasmania on the feast of St Teresa 1940, which was the day that I was born. We both arrived in Devonport, and have been constant observers of each other from the beginning. It is possible that the Cabbage White knows more about me than I know about it. I have a photograph of myself with a cloud of Cabbage Whites. I am three and I am standing among the cabbages in my maternal grandmother's garden, wearing the blue dress with the white edges that my grandmother knitted for me for Christmas. As these were the days before colour photography, the blue of my dress and the blue-green of the cabbages are tinted with inks. My hair is the colour of butter, and my shoes are magical red. The butterflies are untouched by the tinter's brush so that they possess a quality of ethereal purity which is lacking in the coloured areas of the picture. I have always been pleased that I had a grandmother who had Cabbage Butterflies in her cabbages. And I have the photograph to prove it. It was taken the day before Christmas, and on Christmas Day my grandmother died.

The night before they buried her, she came to me as I lay sleeping. She had taken by then the form of the smallest British butterfly, the Small Blue, so often found near warm and sunny grass slopes and in hollows. She was like a forget-me-not. She alighted on my quilt and smiled at me, sweetly, as she always smiled. And all she said was one word. This almost shocked me at the time, because she was a magger, like my mother. She had no doubt trained my mother. She smiled at me as she said:

"Listen."

A Taste of Earth

Holding close the inert, heavy body, I bend over her head and take a deep breath, drawing into my mouth some strands of golden hair: dead hair that has a taste of earth. This taste of earth and of death, and this weight on my heart, is all I have left of you Yvonne de Galais, so ardently sought, so deeply loved . . .

Le Grand Meaulnes, Alain-Fournier

. . . drawing into my mouth some strands of hair: dead hair that has a taste of earth.

Strands of dead hair caught on living lips. The image chilled me when I first read the words. It chills and fascinates me yet.

When I read fiction I want the words to take my spirit into the places beneath the surface of the everyday world. I want the freshness of dreams to be again revealed to me. I want to know the loveliness and terror of what lies beyond the last star, of what lies cradled sweetly in the blood and juices of the human heart. I long to feel the shock when the green sword of the tulip spikes the damp soil, feel the blissful impact of the truth, see the glint, the glimmer, the shimmer of another reality. I desire to be enchanted by the words, to be awakened to the visions and melodies of the writer. I want to feel the anguish and exhilaration of the fiction writer's power to create and destroy. The ideas of creation and destruction haunt me, and I trace this haunting back, back into bright memory.

33

I remember when my mother used to take me to the cemetery.

When there were trams in Launceston, the line ended at the cemetery gates, at the top of a gentle slope. On each side of the tram-line was a row of pine trees that formed a sombre tunnel through which the tram would glide. The cemetery was always called just "Carr Villa" and the words stood for something terrible. My mother and I would go to Carr Villa to put fresh flowers on the family grave. I thought of it as my grandmother's grave, although in it were buried my grandfather and my uncle, both of whom had died before I was born.

Behind the grave was a row of pine trees, and low clipped hedges of rosemary rambled along the edges of the gravel paths. The smell of pine and rosemary, and the smell of corruption, are therefore linked.

At the end of the hedge near my grandmother's grave was a tap. My mother and I would empty the vase, pouring the stale, smelling water into the drain under the tap. Strands of brown, slimy, translucent leaves caught on the grating and slid off as the water drained away. The vase that we were emptying was made of pottery. It was tall, glazed with splashes of prussian blue and yellow ochre. There was always the chance that it would be stolen from the grave, or that one day it would be knocked over and broken. But it was a matter of pride that there must be a real vase on the grave, not a jam-jar. My mother turned the tap on hard. The sound of the water rushing into the vase was to me like a picture, and like a statement going straight from the tap to my heart. In my mother there was always a strange loneliness. As the water gushed into the vase from the tarnished tap by the sinister smell of the drain and the leaves of the rosemary hedge, I knew and partly understood that loneliness.

It was a big old beautiful grave, the surface covered with raked pebbles flecked grey and white and black. In front of the marble headstone was a bouquet of china flowers, white as doves, beneath a glass dome, all sacred to the memory of John Henry, Geoffrey, and Ellen Margaret. Ellen Margaret died when I was three.

I used to see her standing in her kitchen in a dark dress, wearing a navy-blue apron and holding a loaf of bread against her bosom. With a big bone-handled knife she slapped the butter onto the cut end of the loaf, and then she sawed off a slice of buttered bread, cutting in towards her body. Behind her was a mantelpiece from which hung a fringe of burgundy velvet bobbles. Above the mantelpiece in a particular pool of gloom hung an oval picture of the luscious, threatening, beloved Sacred Heart.

He faced the open back door through which could be seen a field of marigolds and, beyond the marigolds, in the cabbages with the white moths, me.

My mother would let me stand on the pebbles of the grave to arrange the flowers in the vase. The pebbles shifted and crunched and shuffled under my shoes.

I was bending over to put marigolds from Ellen's garden into a vase. I began to dissolve until I became a wisp of pointed ectoplasm spearing the surface of the grave which sucked me into itself. Then I stood again in my own cool surprised flesh beside the huge vase of marigolds.

There must be a name for the kind of floor that looks like chips of marble jumbled up together and polished. Smooth shiny floor like a certain kind of sausage. Sometimes it is pinkish, and other times it is grey-blue. The floor of the viewing-room at the back of the funeral parlour is that sort of floor, grey-blue.

In the room there is nothing except the coffin, lit by fluorescent light. It is night. I have come by plane from another city. The lid of the coffin covers most of the body, but I can see my father's head, like wax, with the skull almost visible. He rests in white satin. I kiss him goodbye, and he is not just cold; he is frozen. I suppose the satin stirs with the appearance of breathing because the body is packed in dry ice. I have a cheap camera in my handbag and take a photograph. The click of the camera sounds very loud.

Then there is nothing to do but leave. The tired attendant, who is wearing a navy-blue cardigan, lets me out by the side door

marked "Family". I imagine him going back into the viewing-room.
Is it his job now to screw down the lid? He turns out the light, shuts
the door, and goes to his office. He has a mug of coffee and a cigarette and reads the newspaper. Does he have to stay awake all
night? Does he keep vigil in his cardigan in the quiet building?
Perhaps he would have a video to wile away the hours; a heater and
some comfortable slippers.

In my hotel room I cannot sleep. I too read the newspaper. The
attendant and I are both reading the *National Times on Sunday*, both
reading about Graeme Blundell and women, and something by D. J.
O'Hearn. There is heated carpet on the floor of the bedroom, and in
the bathroom there are heated orange tiles. I drink tea, and listen
to a water-wheel which turns outside my window. When the man in
the navy-blue cardigan and I have completed our vigils, we fold our
newspapers and go our separate and yet still common ways.

He opens the doors for the funeral director and his assistants.
I buy bunches of daffodils to take to the church.

The cars are large grey ones, and seem to slide along the road.
I remember that my father's family used to train the black horses for
these same funeral people.

The floor of the church is wooden, ancient. Faces I have not
seen for thirty years speak to me, and as I look at them, in the sunlight of the funeral, their years dissolve; I know them, and they are
young again.

A machine has dug a deep hole in the orange clay of the cemetery, and the coffin fits perfectly into the space which is edged with
green carpet. Next the carpet is removed and the machine dumps
earth back into the hole. The mound is covered with flowers which
are by now slightly damaged because they have been handled and
arranged several times.

I go back to the airport where the floor of the toilet is the same
as the floor of the viewing-room. I fly home. I take the film to the
chemist to have it developed and printed. A few days pass and I am
so busy I don't get back to the chemist. I think of the photograph I
took in the viewing-room. It is in its orange envelope, standing on
edge with all the other orange envelopes.

The chemist has recently had new red carpet laid on the floor of the shop. When I pick up the prints, I get two of each, and a family photo album.

I sit by the river and peel back the plastic film from the sticky pages of the album. Then I place the photos on the cardboard and cover them with the plastic. Here and there ridges and bubbles form and will not be smoothed away. The first picture is the one of my father in the coffin. His eyes are shut. I realise that the night in the funeral parlour was the first time I ever stood and stared at his sleeping face. Now I can look at it whenever I want to.

As I watch the water, I imagine peeling back the plastic from the first page, picking off the picture of that dead man, tearing it into four pieces, and dropping them into the water. They will float on the top of the ripples for a little while, then separate. Then they drift back together, forming the image just beneath the surface. They undulate, sink.

It is getting dark. I sit on the damp grass and stare down at the water until, by the interplay of light and shadow, a fleet of bobbing ducks moves across the ruffled surface.

Higher Animals

Cold-blooded killing within a species is rare among most higher animals. —Patricia Pitman*

I told them to run across the open field, and first of all I shot Shaun. He fell on his face in the long grass, and Ryan and Danielle just kind of stopped. I reloaded and got Ryan when he was running towards me. But Danielle was screaming and running all over the place. I hit her in the back and she kind of rose in the air like a ballet dancer—and stayed there. —Barry Williams

I don't really know why Barry Williams ended up shooting his children as they ran across a field. I went to school with Barry, and when I opened the paper and read about what he had done, I started to try and remember anything I knew about him, or anything I had been told. There wasn't much. But when someone you used to see every day as a child turns out to commit a triple murder, you try to trace the story back, piecing together the fragments, hoping to make sense of the tragedy.

I can't make any sense out of it of course, but if I put down some of the facts, I might start getting somewhere.

Barry married Leanne Shepherd, and I know some things about Leanne that not many people realize. She looks completely ordinary, and always did the most ordinary things, yet for some rea-

---

*From *Encyclopaedia of Murder*, Colin Wilson and Patricia Pitman (eds.), Pan Books, 1984

son she has always been haunted by fears of disease and death. She told me once when we were nine that she had a tumour on the brain and had been given a month to live. Six weeks at the very most, she said. We were standing in the sand underneath the monkey bars in the playground at school. When I think about it now, I can see Barry Williams playing marbles in the dirt on the other side of the hedge, but that is really only my imagination.

I have got one clear memory of Barry at school. I was a better reader than he was, and I had to listen to him. The reading-book was full of warnings about getting wet, cold, injured, tired, or sad. I had to teach Barry the word "scissors" so that he could read: *Do not cut yourself with the scissors, Roy. The points are sharp.*

Getting back to Leanne and her imaginary illness. She was never really ill, but just completely obsessed by disease and death. And her mother, Deirdre, spent a lot of time thinking about refrigerators.

Deirdre Shepherd assessed every large sum of money by the number and quality of refrigerators it would buy. When she married Dominic he had just won some fabulous amount at the races, and so he bought her a Silent Knight which, over the years, developed a louder and louder voice and gradually lost the ability to keep things cold. In summer it growled like a vigilant watchdog. A pool of smelly water collected on the floor around it, and Deirdre would fold up old bath towels which she placed around the edges to stop the water from making a river across the kitchen and out onto the back verandah. The floorboards began to rot.

Two hundred dollars, she said when the man over the road died and left two hundred dollars to the Salvation Army. *Now that would make a very nice down-payment on a General Electric. Yet the Kelvinator is probably a better proposition just now.* She would sort of juggle with the words *Westinghouse, Frigidaire, Malley's Whirlpool.* She imagined a truck from Maxwell's stopping at the front gate. Then a huge cardboard carton with strips of heavy tape around it would kind of drift up the path and down the hall. What brand was going to be inside it? *What about Electrolux?*

Leanne was Deirdre's youngest daughter. I think she was her favourite. Leanne got engaged to Barry the year Piping Lane won the Melbourne Cup. Deirdre had five dollars on Piping Lane at 40–1, and when she collected her winnings she said, in a voice that had no trace of excitement, perhaps because she had said the words so often before in dream-rehearsal for this moment, *That will make a very nice down-payment on the fridge for Leanne and Barry*. Guided by Deirdre the expert, the couple chose a Frigidaire. Deirdre had her hair done for the wedding.

It was a big wedding with five bridesmaids and a sit-down dinner for a hundred and twenty at Camelot. Leanne's bouquet shook the whole time in church. I met Leanne in the supermarket not long after the wedding, and she told me it wasn't the usual wedding-day nerves. She said she was pretty sure she had leukaemia, and she knew she was going to die before too long. She would never live to have children, and Barry would be alone in the flat with the wedding presents and the Frigidaire. Of course it didn't work out like that at all.

You would never have thought, to look at Leanne, that she had these ideas. The whole thing with disease might have started when she had very bad headaches as a child. She was sure she would soon be dead from cancer of the brain, just as she told me. But the headaches faded and were replaced by pains in the legs. These pains she attributed to cancer of the bone. Then came cancer of the larynx, the stomach, the ovaries, the skin, and finally the lungs. By the time she was walking down the aisle beside her father, she was due for the fatal bout of leukaemia.

What she actually got was life in the flat with Barry. There was the Frigidaire and a daily phone-call from Deirdre.

One time I was there when the phone rang, and Barry said, *That'll be Piping Lane with a new fridge for you, I expect.* And then Leanne said, *One of these days I'm going to take the kids and go back to Mum's.* All Barry said was, *Make it soon, and be sure to take the fucking fridge while you're about it.*

Of course that's only the bare bones of it all. But it's a bit more than you get in the paper when you read the story about a father of three who shot his children when his wife was visiting her mother.

I told them to run across the open field, he said.

Kay Petman's Coloured Pencils

1
WATCHING FROM ABOVE

This was in the time when families had only one car. After breakfast the fathers would drive to work in the cars, the children would catch the bus to school, and the mothers would do the breakfast dishes. There was a sort of whine the cars made as they arrived home in the early evening and were locked up in the garages for the night. Each woman was sensitive to the whine of her husband's car, and when she heard it she would take off her apron, hang the tea-towel on the hook, and put on an oven mitt. For now it was time to take the dinner from the oven. There were sounds of the gate being closed behind the car, the gentle chatter of the engine as the car was being eased into the garage, then the click and grind as the garage doors were closed. Gods watching from above could see through the roofs of the houses as if they were glass, and could see the mothers putting the meat and vegetables on the tables, see the children in their bedrooms closing their history textbooks before washing their hands for the evening meal.

2
WHEN A GIRL MARRIES

The gods saw two rows of houses on either side of a gravel street. This was after the Second World War, before television, before the pill. Some houses had cellars where boxes of faded photographs and broken kitchen chairs gathered mould; some had little attics where trunks of crumpled ball-gowns collected dust. Between the attics and the cellars were rooms full of everyday life, busy with pop-up toasters, vacuum cleaners, pressure cookers, and radios that told the story. Each house was surrounded by a garden. In the front there were lawns with flower borders; at the back there was a lemon tree and a circular clothes-line. Next to most back fences was a little hen house, and beside some of the hen houses were the trap-doors leading to the trenches which the fathers had dug for the safety of the families in the event of an invasion of Japanese.

3
NUMBER TEN

Jack and Margaret Petman lived at number ten. They had a daughter called Kay who was rather pretty. She looked quite good in her high school dress. This dress was pale blue with a white collar and was worn with a panama hat and white gloves. Kay always got good marks in English, history, and art. She was going to art school when she was seventeen. But first she was going to be a deb. It was one of the things her mother had been looking forward to for years.

Apples kept well in the trench.

Kay would sit at the desk in her bedroom drawing the designs for her deb dress with inks and coloured pencils. The background of the drawing was a dream forest of carefully drawn leaves and bright flowers against which the white spun sugar of the dress blazed and sparkled. Kay put some of the designs in her satchel. She was going to take them to school where she would show them to Miss Battista, the art teacher.

4
DANGER

Francesca Battista was exotic. She was little, thirty, dark, beautiful, foreign, unmarried, mysterious, artistic, and Roman Catholic. She also drove a car.

When Margaret Petman was doing the sheets and towels in

her washing machine, and when Jack Petman was checking the
level of the brine for the icy-poles at the ice-cream factory,
Francesca was squeezing bright oil paints onto palettes for the girls
in the art room. Kay watched as the soft snake of yellow ochre slide
onto the wood.

"Miss Battista, can I show you the designs for my dress?"

When Francesca saw the drawings she decided to save Kay
before it was too late.

5
THE INVITATION

So while Margaret hoses the leaves from the crazy paving,
Francesca says to Kay:

"Would you like to bring all your designs to my house on
Saturday?"

Kay goes funny inside with surprise and pleasure at the invitation and says:

"I'll ask."

They are making pineapple icy-poles at the factory today.

6
IDEA

After the ball, and after she leaves school and before she gets
married, Kay could get a job in the office at the ice-cream factory.

7
SATURDAY

Kay is allowed to go to the art teacher's house with the drawings for the deb dress. Margaret reminds her that the ball is in six
months time and everything will have to be settled before too long.
There is also the question of a partner. Is she going to get round to
asking Robert Scott quite soon because if she doesn't hurry up somebody else will ask him? Somebody such as Mary Robinson for
instance. And has Kay heard that Mary got ninety-one in her grade
five piano exam?

Jack is mowing the lawn.

8
THEY TALK ABOUT DREAMS

In Miss Battista's flat all the little windows are open and calico curtains with borders of blue flowers flap a bit in the wind. Insects fly in and settle as Miss Battista admires their colour and form. On a pale table a yellow bowl of daisies. A white cat. The smell of expensive perfume. Huge velvet cushions. Miss Battista is cleaning her teeth.

They have cakes and coffee and talk about French poetry. And Botticelli. And the *Divine Comedy*. And the stars. The dresses Kay has drawn are very pretty. So are the forests. Where did she get the forests from? From dreams. They talk about dreams.

Miss Battista sketches as she talks. She hums. Kay is drawing too. There is a sweet scratch scratch of their pencils on their drawing blocks.

"May I?" says Miss Battista and corrects the line of the daisy Kay is drawing.

9
QUERY FROM GODS

"Is that how it happened, then? How Kay Petman stepped out one Saturday straight off the straight and narrow path of her mother's crazy paving, and down among the primroses, waving goodbye to Robert Scott as he waltzes in the moonlight with Mary Robinson in his arms? Such a simple little thing, so sweet and very Italian, and she lifts her finger and Kay Petman says 'Oh, yes yes, I never wanted to be a deb at the Masonic Ball. I'll get a job and save up and go to Italy.'"

10
THE SHINY SKIN OF THE EARTH

Jack is cleaning the car. And waxing it. He does a thorough job.

The three-year-old girl at number fourteen has sliced the top off her finger with a wire for cutting cheese.

Kay goes into Francesca's laundry to wash her hands. A little picture is stuck crookedly into a corner of the window frame. It shocks her. Black madonna in jewelled robe; black child. Their crowns are held up by angels in short skirts. Kay stares at the picture with her mouth half open. In what is known as a split second she sees some bright thing springing from the darkest cracks in the bleeding earth. The rocks are ripped apart and an unearthly light screams swiftly in across the light of day. She washes her hands and returns to her drawing.

"There is something the matter," says Francesca.

Mozart piano concertos playing softly.

"Nothing the matter," says Kay.

(I have seen something black and terrible. If I go back to the laundry to look at it again, will it still be there, staring so sadly, looking through the skin of my eyes into the stream of my blood, the look swirling round and round in me until my heart is pierced and split with slashes, cut with a burning sword? Or if I go back, will the picture be gone? Did it bubble out from the shiny skin of the earth, stick to the window for just a minute, and then dissolve into the air, sail through the little invisible cracks in the ceiling of the laundry?)

"In Italy," says Francesca, "the sky is quite a different blue, you know."

Margaret Petman is peeling parsnips.

"I had better be going home now," says Kay.

Jack is putting away the car.

"Come again another time. What about next Saturday?"

"I have to go to the first rehearsal for the ball."

Francesca's eyes are brown as the eyes of a deer.

Mary Robinson is speaking to Robert Scott's mother. Robert will be home from football soon.

Kay lines up all her pencils in the tin.

The Right Stuff

You can't book into a motel under a false name any more. They want to see your driver's licence or your Bankcard.

—What about people who haven't got those things—whispered a little voice to Caroline Jessup. And Caroline whispered back.

—There are no such people.

Caroline discovered all this the night she went to the Whispering Pines with Graeme Frith. She discovered other things as well.

Caroline and Peter Jessup had been married for nearly ten years when this happened. The twins were away on a school camp; Peter was interstate on business; Caroline was a bit bored and lonely and was looking at the imported cheeses in the supermarket. There was Graeme choosing fish fingers.

"Hello, Caroline. Long time no see."

And it went on from there. He came home with her and carried the bags of shopping from the station wagon to the kitchen. He had forgotten by then all about his fish fingers. They had coffee in the kitchen and she showed him the fruit trees Peter had planted in the back courtyard, and the roses she had put at the front.

"You ought to have a Josephine Bruce. Nice deep red. Jillian was very fond of Josephine Bruce. You remind me a little of Jillian actually, Caroline. You realize we've split up, Jillian and I."

"I had heard."

Well, one thing led to another, and Graeme and Caroline ended up back at the supermarket where they bought a Josephine Bruce and something to kill the aphids and something else to deal with scale.

"This stuff here is good for curly leaf. Does Peter get curly leaf? On the peaches?"

Caroline didn't know the answer to that, but they got some of the stuff anyway. This time Graeme carried the bags from the station-wagon to the garden shed, and in the garden shed he took Caroline's hand and kissed it. She was half surprised but rather pleased. With her other hand she stroked his face, and then he kissed her and they decided to plant the Josephine Bruce there and then.

"She'll have to go between Princess Elizabeth and Charles de Gaulle."

"Right."

And Graeme thrust the spade into the earth with his foot. Healthy little worms wriggled out of the clumps of soil.

Graeme and Caroline gradually worked their way around the garden and around the house, and when they were back in the kitchen drinking their fourth cup of coffee, Graeme said,

"You're a sweet girl, Caroline. I always thought you were a sweet girl."

And Caroline said nothing but kissed him again and then they both looked towards the bedroom.

"Oh no," said Caroline, "I could never do that. Not in our bedroom at least. And besides, Peter could come home at any moment."

Graeme had not realized that she (the sweet girl) would be so difficult. But he could see that she meant what she said.

"We could go to your place?"

She looked at him.

(My God, she doesn't realize I share the boarding house with six other marital cast-offs. What about the phone that never works because it's been ripped out of the wall? How would poor old Josie

Bruce go in the front garden with the broken chairs and the old mat-
tresses? Caroline reminds me just that little bit of Jillian. Wouldn't it
be nice to get into a little bit of Jillian? Rather nice to hurt her a frac-
tion too. You're a complex person, Graeme. Go ahead, son.)

"I've got a better idea," said Graeme. "Let's go to the
Whispering Pines."

A little shock and thrill ran through Caroline. She had never
gone to a motel with a man. Graeme watched her as she packed her
suitcase. She reminded him of his daughter when she used to get her
things ready to go to kindergarten. It was a small metal case, white
with scarlet dots.

"You don't need all that stuff, Caroline. They don't expect you
to have a case. Necessarily."

"But we will stay the night. Actually stay the night . . . ?" He
looked at her with one eyebrow raised.

"Won't we?" asked Caroline.

"If you like. You can have breakfast in bed and a swim in the
pool."

(Already I am sorry the idea of the Whispering Pines crossed
my lips. Caroline has turned out, quite suddenly, to be incredibly
stupid and boring. Who could have imagined? What if I took this
sweet boring girl with her kindergarten supplies of creams and
lotions and underwear down to the garden shed. Might work? She
might just go for it there among the packets of Defender and the
cans of Slay-Afe. No? No Graeme. This one wants to put her red and
white spotted suitcase into the boot of your Toyota and go to the
Whispering Pines and be Mrs Frith. Graeme, how did all this happen? There you were, innocently standing by the frozen fish in the
bit next to the imported cheeses when bang! up comes this pretty
little woman in a yellow track suit and says, "We are going to the
Whispering Pines together. Get your things, Graeme.")

She sang along with the radio in the car on the mountain road.
Graeme joined in. He could throw himself into these events, knew
how to make the best of the most unpromising circumstances. And
after a while, there, at the end of the long mountain road, was the
Whispering Pines, nestling among the mysterious trees like a house

in a fairy tale where they take Bankcard, American Express, Diner's Club . . .

Graeme signed them in, the Friths, produced his licence, and carried the silly little suitcase to the room.

(God, Graeme, this room is so much like every motel room in the world it's funny. There's the brown carpet, the orange bedspread, the orange and yellow curtains, the picture of a horse's head, and the gurgling fridge full of little bottles of whisky and gin. You must be nuts. Look at this bloody woman unpacking the spotty suitcase. Out comes the romantic negligée, peach satin. It truly is peach satin.)

Graeme thinks fondly of the torn lace curtain, grey, on his window in the boarding house. He likes to lie on his poor sagging bed reading *Mad* and *Time* and the *Gun Journal*, and watching the shadows as they creep through the curtain.

(But something is wrong now, Graeme old son. Are they tears falling on the satin negligée? Yes, they are.)

"What's up?"

"I don't know what to do."

"About what?"

"The man. The man at the desk. He lives in our street. He knows me. He knows who I am."

"He didn't even look at you. Didn't even see you. They don't look at people you know."

"Of course they do. He did. He was pretending not to. He's probably ringing his wife now. Telling her. They're the Dobsons in number five. I knew this would happen."

She stopped weeping and looked at him coldly. Then she brushed the teardrops from the peach satin and put it back in the case.

"Take me home. I'm sorry. I can't go through with this."

Graeme could not believe his ears.

"Look come and get in the spa. You'll feel better."

She gave him a withering look. Graeme withered. He knew when not to argue with people. He took her home. Down the mountain they went. It was dark by now. They stopped once and Graeme got some Kentucky Fried Chicken which they ate in the car, chatting politely about take-away food. She would have preferred McDonald's. They had no choice. It was Kentucky Fried or nothing out here in the middle of nowhere.

It was nearly midnight when they got back to the house. There was a smell of freshly turned earth, and no sign of Peter.

"He won't be back until tomorrow night now. He will have stopped somewhere on the way."

So Graeme went inside and spent the night with Caroline who, strangely enough, had stopped protesting. She did not, he noticed, bother about the peach satin negligée. She made breakfast for him in the morning, and they spent a delightful hour in the spa. When he left, she said to ring her some time. No harm in that, thought Graeme, now that we have broken the ice. I'll probably take her up on that.

The twins came back from camp with colds; nothing was ever heard from the Dobsons at number five, although Caroline felt that Mrs Dobson looked at her inquisitively in the delicatessen. When Peter found the stuff for curly leaf he was really pleased and said,

"You're a fantastic woman, Caroline. I've been looking everywhere for this stuff."

Buttercup and Wendy

This is the legend of Wendy Trull who was the prettiest girl in Tasmania between 1955 and, say, 1959. A long time to hold any title, particularly that of beauty queen.

When you see a beginning like that, you know that Wendy must either triumph over terrible odds and end up as the wife of a diplomat, or she must be doomed. Will Wendy be found at the bottom of the cliff, broken like a wax doll, with strange juices oozing out, and her ears in a paper bag, you wonder; or will she have a wedding in the Cathedral, and an ironing lady, and a second house at the beach, perhaps even a third in the mountains and a flat in London? And for the children a nanny who is more like a second mother to them than a servant. What is going to happen to Wendy?

Wendy lived with her mother and father and brother and sisters in a reasonably nice house with wide verandas on Windmill Hill. The needles from the pine trees collected on the verandas, and one of Wendy's jobs was to sweep them up and put them in the incinerator. Wendy's granny lived in a grim old terrace house in a poorer part of the town. She kept the brass doorknob on the front door gleaming, and in the passage, just inside the door, she kept a cow. You opened the door, and there, standing sadly on the pink and green lino, was a brown and white cow. Cows' eyes look very big indeed when you see them up close in the narrow dimness of an entrance hall.

If there are motifs and links in the lives of people, then the presence of the cow in her granny's passage can be related to the presence of a secret lover in Wendy's attic. There were many years between the cow and the lover, but Buttercup, certainly an unusual pet, is somehow linked in Wendy's life to the man in the attic.

The attic, not yet brushed by the jacaranda which would be there by the time Wendy came, was waiting for Wendy's lover at the top of a house which was waiting for Wendy. Across the sea from Wendy's island, in a part of the world called Kew (thousands of miles from London, for Wendy will not roam too far), there stood a warm brick house with a fancy wooden veranda and an attic. The attic was full of attic secrets and forgotten attic dreams.

The family who lived there, in this long time before Wendy got there, were the Fagans: Old Missus, her son, his wife, and their fat sons who spent many wet afternoons in the attic where they read comics, did unspeakable things, and imagined that they were spying on the girls in the garden next-door. The jacarandas dropped their soft blue blossoms onto the grass where the girls sat painting their toe-nails and rubbing each other with oil. Much of what they did was done for the entertainment of the Fagans in the attic.

When Old Missus died her son sold the house which then had a succession of rather careless owners, one of whom put an Alsatian in the fowl-house instead of hens. Sadder and sadder grew the house as it waited for Wendy. Would she never come? Somebody, inspired perhaps by the trees on the other side of the fence, planted the jacaranda which was going to be there when Wendy arrived and signed the contract to buy the house.

"It's very run down," said her friends.

"Yes," said Wendy, "but I'm going to do it up."

Although no cow had ever roamed the front hall of the house, there seemed to be some faint melody which sang in

Wendy's heart of the memory of her granny. The lino in the front parlour was pink and green. If Wendy changed this house, made it smell of paint and disinfectant, would she change the fact that her granny had lived with a cow? If she tidied the house, she might tidy the memory.

Before the jacaranda was planted, when Wendy was at high school, and was the prettiest girl in town, she went around with the boy who was the best tennis player, for his age, in the state. He was called Michael—a boy with ice-blue eyes and a very attractive laugh. Michael and Wendy went together to school dances to which he wore a white sports coat with a pink carnation, and she wore an orange skirt beneath which undulated a vast white petticoat edged with rope. They went together to school picnics, and to the pictures on Saturdays. In school plays, she was Portia to his Shylock, Eliza to his Higgins.

The legend said that he spent every second night, just about, in her bedroom at the back of the house on Windmill Hill. However, the truth is that he went there once, and they were both so terrified of being discovered by her father that they didn't enjoy themselves at all, except for when Wendy got some licorice straps out of a drawer and they ate them. He did not go to her bedroom again. Instead, he would borrow his father's car and take Wendy to the drive-in. The car was a big black Chevrolet which had cost, said the legend, well over eleven hundred pounds. The back seat was fairly comfortable. Naturally, the legend said that they went all the way in the back of the Chev, but that isn't true either.

They left school, and the end of the chapter came when Wendy was a deb. Michael, wearing a dinner suit, was her partner, and they were the most beautiful couple on the floor. Wendy's dress was made by old Mrs Winter, the local maker of debs' dresses. Three times a week for four weeks, Wendy stood on Mrs Winter's dining-room table in a trance as Mrs Winter took pins from her mouth and made them go "tuck tuck" in the white silk. Wendy wanted to look like the most fabulous fairy on the top of the most incredible Christmas tree. And she did.

Then after that, Michael went to Hobart to study the Law,

and Wendy went to Kew—oh, distant and foreign land of Australia where people ate ravioli—to train to be a kindergarten teacher. She had pastel twin-sets, and pleated skirts, smart blazers, and pearls. She was a good student, and strove to look like a model from *Seventeen*. She forgot Buttercup for the time being, keeping her thoughts fixed on respectability, a certificate in kindergarten teaching, and marriage to the right man. And so Michael receded. It had not taken much, just a strip of water, to sever the bonds between Michael and Wendy. Michael continued to play tennis, seduced the professor's daughter, failed first year, and crashed his father's car.

Legend suggested that if Michael had stayed with Wendy, he might have been all right. As it was, he went into his father's firm and developed an interest in racing. Before long, he was in debt to the bookmakers, stole money from his father and ended up in prison, his ice-blue eyes staring at a window through which he could not see the sky. Prison did not improve him, however, and when he was released, he set about stealing some more money and went back to jail. He seemed to have set himself a pattern for life.

Wendy, in due course, became the director of a kindergarten. It was in a fashionable and wealthy suburb where the parents and children were happy with Wendy, and Wendy was happy with them. When she read to the children stories about cows called Daisy or Buttercup, she no longer thought of her granny. She would take the children to farmyards, and occasionally the huge brown eyes of a solemn cow would bring back to her a picture of the pink and green lino, and of her granny's fingers as they stroked Buttercup's ears. But this was rare. She had left it all behind her; she was a career-woman. Once upon a time, in the days of the pastel twin-sets, one of her aims had been to marry. To marry the right man. Ah, but alas, she had not met the right man. The ambition faded; she had love affairs, some happy, some sad.

It was a renovator's opportunity with an original fireplace, the house in Kew. Wendy hired a truck and took the fowl-house and the contents of the attic, as well as some cupboards which smelt of vomit, and an ice-chest full of spiders, to the tip. Then, with the help of a builder and a plumber and a painter, she began the renovations. Most of the floor she covered with carpet, thick and royal blue. Even the little stairs which wound up to the attic were blue, woolly under Wendy's bare feet. It was up this little winding staircase that the secret lover crept.

Wendy had not seen Michael for twenty years when he escaped from prison and found her in her back garden, sitting underneath the jacaranda with her bare feet in the grass.

Pause and picture that.

One Sunday afternoon, Miss Wendy Trull is reading *The White Hotel* on the grass at the back of her place, when a tired man with ice-blue eyes and a dirty t-shirt comes up the path. She shuts her book, flicks a blue blossom from her skirt, and invites the man into the kitchen for a drink. He has a shower, and is never seen again.

It was, in many ways, quite a good arrangement for both of them. Michael, seeking, it would seem, one kind of prison or another, had found one to his taste.

Wendy was quite used to making rules for her kindergarten, and so she easily drew up the rules of the attic. There would be no light allowed between 5 pm and 8 am. The cupboard must remain in front of the window. Michael must never come downstairs unless Wendy came to get him. The gate to the back garden was blocked off so that anybody who came to the house had to ring the front doorbell. Michael knew that when the bell rang, he must stay quiet until Wendy came to say that the visitor had gone. Wendy bought an exercise bike and another TV.

And so, in their attic dreamland, where they made love in the afternoons and early mornings, and where they ate delicious snacks and licorice straps, they lived happily ever after, the prettiest girl in Tasmania and her childhood sweetheart.

Wendy used to think about the reality of the "ever after". Would he die first? Would they commit suicide? When? How did people decide those things? Would the headlines in cheap newspapers say:

ATTIC PRISONER KINDERGARTEN TEACHER
SUICIDE
or
CHILDHOOD SWEETHEARTS DIE IN PACT?

As she thought about how it would be, life went on as usual. The biggest difference to Wendy's life, outside the attic that is, was the fact that she could never go away for holidays. She felt, however, no need of holidays, having as she did such an interesting home-life.

"But when are you going to Venice?" they said. "You always told us you were going to go to Venice."

In the summer the jacaranda bloomed. Soft blue blossoms with no perfume against a harsh blue sky. The branches were dark like ink, scratched in twisted twig patterns. And around the branches, in clouds like moths, hovered the jacaranda flowers, blue
and blue
and blue.

Seeking Its Level

SB, 2BR house, truly immac, WWC,
LU gar, int facils, handy trpt,
will impress, rustic setting,
bond, refs, lease.

Anna Pavlova Flower, known to the world as Anne, signed the lease on the eve of her thirtieth birthday. Her references were excellent.

She moved in just after Christmas, a good tenant in a rustic setting, teacher of physical education at a very good high school, truly immac.

On the first night, when the bath water had all drained away there was a dirty ring around the bath and a greenish stain along the bottom. Anna Pavlova retained from childhood a horror of the noise which water made as it ran down the plug-hole. And it was fascinating the way the water disappeared. One minute the bath was full of milky-looking water, and then with an agonized cry and a fast and bubbling whirlpool, and a last gust of Crabtree and Evelyn citrus soap, the water was gone, the bath dividing the waters below from the waters above.

Across the metal grid in the plug-hole there was a little woven mat of hair and dirt and slime.

Anna Pavlova stood in the bathroom with the black rubber plug lying in her hand, the silver beady chain looped across her fingers. She let the chain go and the plug swung down clonk into the bath. Wouldn't it make a terrible noise if you got into the empty bath with your overcoat on and shot yourself. Through the head, say. Wouldn't the blood look bright and dark and terrible splattered across the old white enamel, dripping down the ring of dirt, draining away where the water had gone, sliding over the green stain, snaking into the underworld, seeking its level, doing it with physics.

Outside the window was the rustic setting.

There would be Donald, who taught physics to the bigger boys at the high school, sitting on the old-world seat, smoking a cigarette which he had just rolled himself in that slow but busy way he had. There were leaves floating on the surface of the pond. Huge and round as a fairy tale, a spider's web hung between two bushes, beaded with moisture, big as a wheel. Anna Pavlova needed to buy some secateurs because she couldn't cut the lilac with her scissors. She would have to go to the hardware shop and get some nice new secateurs with red paint on the handles, and a little black lever to push back and forth with her thumb. Then what if she got cancer and they put her in the hospital and kept her there and she couldn't get out, eleven storeys up in the air, and they sliced off bits of her and burned other bits away and there was practically nothing left, and the secateurs just stayed in the lock-up garage and rusted away. She would be dead in some terrible morgue and people would come to look at her, but they would not know to rescue the secateurs.

She wound a towel around her head and dried between her toes. With one hand on the towel-rail, she did some ballet exercises, just like always, remembering the hard, supple body of the man who used to teach her ballet when she was fifteen, and the way he used to say never waste a towel-rail . . . stretch!

Anna Pavlova stretched. Plié . . . and str-etch!

Ivan used to teach ballet in the stable at the back of his beautiful old house. Once a year, the students were invited into the house for a glittering Christmas party. Gilt and crystal and statues from Rome. The brocades came from Paris, the mood from the czars. Ivan was a prince.

Never waste a towel-rail.

Treasure the lace handkerchief he gave you when you left to go to teachers' college.

Would Donald ever notice her? Was he going to look up from the pile of physics assignments and notice her. Was he going to say, one pale lilac afternoon in the staff room, let's have a drink after school.

One of these days I'm going to clean the bath properly. If you don't get married by the time you're thirty, you've had it. That's it. All over. What if Donald is at this very moment sitting on some other woman's rustic bench, and that woman is twenty-four, and very, very gifted in physics and football and the arts.

Everybody got married. My sisters are married, and all the girls I went to school with, and just about everyone from college, except for a few over-brainy ones and some who were so incredibly stupid and ugly they have probably been put in a home for the incurably grotesque. All the married ones have got husbands and babies and houses and gardens, and what else did you get, furniture, yes they have their own bookcases and cupboards and bedroom suites and lounge suites and coffee tables and occasional chairs and kitchen tidies. They've got their own houses close to transport and shops and schools. This house doesn't belong to me. The green stain in the bath is not really mine. I am thirty and the house does not belong to me. This is not my garden.

The lilac blooms outside the bathroom window, and it is not mine. And yet I ought to get some secateurs and cut some of the flowers and put them in water. Turn on the tap and get some water from above into the vase beneath. I can take the flowers in my arms and carry them into the house and put them in the biggest blue vase.

Anna Pavlova pulled some flowers off with her hands. The branches broke, leaving untidy jagged edges. If you had a child, it could be running up the street ahead of you, running past the house with the little red letter box and all the flowers, and you could be on your way to the park. The child runs around the corner. You catch up. You go around the corner. The child has gone. Disappeared. Lost child. Beaumont Child, Eloise Child, Azaria Child. Child running over sand; round corner over sand dune into scrub hanging rock open sky heavens open pull out the plug and let the water go and the child. Is gone.

Anna Pavlova looked for the old secateurs in the garage. Packets of dried-up snail bait. Empty seed packets. (In crust-forming soils, cover the seed rows with a layer of old lawn clippings. A fragrant mixture of warm colours including reds, brown, golden-yellow and white. Always cut flowers in cool weather.)

She found an axe and began to attack the trunk of the lilac tree. It took her nearly an hour before the cracked and chipped branches of the lilac lay in weeping heaps on the earth, pale florets fluttering, lying in bruised drifts at her feet.

Donald was not watching her from the rustic seat as she hosed the earth, chasing the little blossoms until they disappeared into a drain. The water soaked into the soil, soaked in and was gone.

Introducing Your Friends

Valerie was most herself when stacking plates. Shining, circular and white, the plates behaved under her hands. Valerie took them, four at a time, between thumb and fingers, and put them with a clinking noise into the cupboard. Her fingernails were painted red, and she had three children. Cheerful men in grey overalls, driving enormous vans, would come to Valerie's house with furniture chosen from bright catalogues. There was a need, in Valerie's life, for an adjective to go with every noun. She had luxurious towels, elegant armchairs, colonial dressers. Her husband was a teacher in a high school; he was handsome, as was right, but had grown perhaps a bit distant from his family as the lounge filled up with fat velvet furniture and as the floor of the family room swam ever deeper with a sea of patchwork cushions and pieces of Lego. Valerie was a nurse.

Every year there was a fête at the children's school and Valerie ran the cake stall. Under a blue tent on the front lawn of the school Valerie bustled about in her red gingham apron, her hair plaited in tight bunches over her ears because it was hot. To say that she bustled might give an idea that she was a bit round or even fat. That is not so, for Valerie, noted for her energy and drive, was almost angular, her skin slightly freckled and stretched across her bones. But she did not move with grace. As one cake was sold she fidgeted with all the others so that the display would look balanced. The cake stall always made heaps of money, and sold out just as the president of the mothers' club was drawing the last raffle for the day.

It was while she was serving on the cake stall that Valerie met Stella. Valerie often watched television, and she had seen Stella in soap operas. And here was Stella (better known to Valerie and the world as Marjory, Mary Ellen, or Sister Veronica) wearing sandals and a white lace dress, buying shortbread, with a pimple on her nose, in Valerie's blue tent.

"Isn't it hot?" said Stella.

"Oh yes," said Valerie. "Would you like a cup of tea?"

"I'd adore that," said Stella.

So there she was, Stella Rees, sitting on the deck chair drinking tea in Valerie Duffy's cake tent.

Stella was three-dimensional after all. White and pink, her flesh curved around her bones; a golden haze dusted her skin. You could walk around her, looking at her from all sides, not having to wait for her to move. Valerie could make Stella turn her head just by saying "Sugar?". And her hair was a great brown bush which frizzed in wild bunches to her shoulders. She must have to wear wigs on telly. Or perhaps this was a wig. Valerie looked closely at the hairline. It was not a wig. Valerie stacked some plates which were all of different shapes so that they made a rather wobbly pile. She did not feel quite herself in the presence of this manifestation of Stella. It was disturbing, just faintly, to be talking to a television actress. Valerie felt as though she had opened the pages of a picture book and the fairies had fluttered out of the pictures at her. She became very matter-of-fact and business-like. She pretended that Stella was not really special, was not the idol of millions of people, but was just a customer drinking tea in the blue tent.

"Did you see the garden stall?" said Valerie.

"No, I'm going there in a minute. I've actually been buying aprons and things for Christmas presents. And the most lovely Red Riding Hood cloaks for my nieces. Look."

From her basket she unfolded two little velvet cloaks.

"Oh," said Valerie, "Felicity made those. I got the material for her at the Buzy Bee. They're nice, aren't they?"

"I think they're just perfect. To tell you the truth, I'd like to have one myself. Perhaps a blue one. What do you think? Does Felicity make big ones?"

"Well you could ask her. I could give you her number if you like. She lives next door to me."

And so it was that Stella met Felicity.

Although Felicity lived in a house which had originally been almost the same as Valerie's, the two houses were now quite different. Valerie's was surrounded by discreet little native shrubs which poked up from a bed of tan bark. Out the back of the house there was a barbecue, a rotary clothes line, a set of garden chairs and a table, a swing, a gum tree and a dog kennel. Felicity's house was covered with passionfruit vines so that people had to bend down to get in the door. There were two hens and a duck, five guinea pigs, three canaries, a cat, a dog, and five children. Unlike Valerie's smart and dusted furniture, Felicity's was all falling to pieces, except for the ancient cupboards and chests which her grandmother had brought from Scotland. These stood, the colour of dark honey, like wise old storytellers amongst the clutter of Felicity's life.

"I see," said Felicity to Stella, "that you must have a cloak the colour of midnight. Blue as heaven."

"Oh yes, yes," said Stella. "Yes. You know exactly."

And so it was that Felicity made the velvet cloak for Stella while Valerie, on her old gold velvet settee, watched as Sister Veronica was persecuted for her views on sex education, and as Marjory made decisions about when to consult the pediatrician and when to take the baby to the hairdresser. There came a special kind of chirruping, it seemed to Valerie, from the house next door whenever Stella was there. Stella brought rabbits for the children, and Spanish combs for Felicity's hair. They could all do with a decent visit to the hairdresser, Stella and Felicity and all the grubby children, thought Valerie.

It was spring when the blue cloak was finished. Under the

apple blossom in Felicity's back garden there was a rickety table and some old cane chairs. Onto the table Felicity spread a lace cloth, and then she brought out the cups from her Auntie Ann in Devon. From her kitchen window, Valerie watched the ritual. Felicity and the brown teapot; Felicity and the sponge cake; Felicity and the ham sandwiches. Then, fighting her way through the passionfruit vine, laughing and doing that special chirrup, came Stella, magnificent in the flowing cloak of deep blue velvet. She ran around the garden like a mad magician, leapt onto a tree stump, and then fluttered down into one of the chairs under the tree. Valerie thought how like ridiculous little children they were. And both of them were forty. If not more. Felicity poured the tea and they both twittered and chattered over their plates of cake.

Valerie went back to her washing up, polishing the plates until they gleamed. She stacked them in the cupboard where they shone like eggs. She took a cup and rinsed a speck from it under the tap and as she looked out of the window onto the scene under the apple tree the cup slipped, broke, and cut her hand. She let the blood drip into the water in the sink. Then she pushed up the window and called out, "Oh Felicity. Hello. Oh sorry, I didn't realize you were in the garden. Have you got a Bandaid? I don't seem to have any, and I've just cut my hand."

So they asked her to join them, and Stella put on the Bandaid, and Valerie felt much better.

The Best Thing to Do

Trevor lived on the edge of the harbour. The house was at the bottom of a long steep slope into which were cut a hundred and twelve steps. In front of the house was a jetty where Trevor often sat to watch the ducks as they swam past. One evening when he was there smoking his pipe and sipping a whisky, he saw two very handsome brown ducks come sailing by. As he watched, they moved off in separate directions. It occurred to Trevor then that he and his wife Alice had drifted apart.

It isn't like it used to be fifteen or so years ago, thought Trevor. Nothing definite has happened, but something has come between Alice and me. Is it just time, the passing of time?

The sharp perfume of orange blossom filled the evening air. It came from Alice's two orange trees which grew on either side of the back door. And there was Alice prodding with a fork the earth and leaves beneath the trees. Could it be snails, she wondered, that were eating the green skins of the young oranges?

"I'm afraid," said Louisa, daughter of Alice and Trevor, "that one night my father will slip on the steps coming home and be killed."

65

"What makes you say that, Louisa?" asked Miss Bibby, student counsellor at Wildwood School.

"Because there are no lights on the steps, and he comes home in the dark."

"Ah," said Miss Bibby, sensing the rest of the story with the nose of the expert. "Why does your father come home in the dark?"

"Well, actually," said Louisa, pausing to purse her lips in preparation for the appalling boldness of the thing she was about to say, "actually, he stays out drinking with the people from the office."

"With the men from the office," said Miss Bibby flatly, inviting with her cool, professional voice, the next confidence.

"Oh, men and ladies," said Louisa.

The poor child, Louisa, usually quite able and accomplished at school, had failed seven out of eight subjects in the term exams and it was Miss Bibby's job to find out why and attempt to intervene. So there it was, thought Laurel Bibby, somewhat disappointed at the ease with which she had extracted the information. But now came the challenge! Laurel Bibby must somehow change the situation.

"And your mother, what does she feel about all this, Louisa?"

"I don't know." Louisa was irritable, miserable. "She doesn't talk to me very much. Neither does he. I don't suppose they even think about me."

"Why do you say that now, Louisa?"

"My mother is always in the garden or on the phone, and my father is always watching television or staring into the water. He sits on the end of the jetty with a glass of whisky and watches the boats, I suppose, and the ducks."

"I see," said Laurel Bibby. And she did.

Many times Louisa went to see Miss Bibby, and they discussed drugs, boys, fashion, and music. What Laurel did then was against her principles; she grew fond of Louisa. She agreed to go home to dinner with her.

"Yes," she said, "yes, Louisa, I believe that would be the best thing to do."

"Oh, yes," she said to Alice, "of course it is snails at the oranges. I get them every year. Pellets are the only thing."

Then as Alice was serving the casserole Trevor came home, and in such a condition that Laurel found it something of a miracle that he had not slipped on the stairs and been killed that very night. He sat down at the table and talked without stopping.

Then suddenly he buried his face in his mashed potatoes.

"It's all right," said Louisa. "He isn't dead, just sleeping."

The poor child. Oh, the foolish, pathetic man. And so handsome. And his talk, non-stop as it was, so very amusing.

The next day, Trevor apologized to Laurel by telephone, and she accepted his invitation to meet him for a cup of coffee. From then on, things never looked back. And Louisa's marks, reflecting her father's happiness, returned to normal.

Laurel began to meet Trevor and the other men and ladies from the office for a drink after work. She felt that she had widened her sphere of influence. She listened, said the others, with such sympathy and advised with such tact.

There were so many challenging problems in the lives of the men and ladies of the office.

"Come home and have supper with me," said Trevor to Laurel. And in a sudden rush of hospitality, he extended the invitation to their companions.

So it was that at a time long after dark a group of laughing, shouting executives and secretaries arrived at the top of the slope.

"You live WHERE, Trevor?"

"Down there. Just down there." He gestured at the cliffside. "Behind that giant palm tree at the bottom, there is my little old stone cottage."

"Can't see a thing. What palm tree? Are you sure you live here?"

"It is surrounded by orange trees and covered with roses. Home. There used to be ducks on the water, but they have drifted away. All drifted away. Deserted."

As Trevor said "deserted", the headlights of a passing truck dazzled him, and he slipped sideways, grabbed for the railing, missed, and slid swiftly down the steps.

● ● ●

"It was horrible. A nightmare. So dark," said Laurel to the teachers at Wildwood. "There was nothing we could do. He lay all twisted up across a crooked step half-way down. A terrible, terrible shock for the family. But Louisa seems to be getting on with her work and is likely to win the scholarship. Alice has the garden. It is common knowledge that Alice and Trevor had more or less drifted apart over the years. But it *was* a terrible tragedy. Being a friend of the family, I know what it meant to them. A tragedy. One doesn't always know *exactly* what is best to do. In a case like that."

Buff Orpington and the Disasters of Middle Life

Carrillo Mean, Californian guru, did not write his definitive work, *Buff Orpington and the Disasters of Middle Life*, until well after Stanford Fox, Melbourne barrister, had suffered some of those disasters.

THE PEOPLE

Stan Fox—a barrister
Maureen—his wife
Melanie—his girl friend
Tony—his partner
Margaret—Tony's second wife
Barbara—Tony's first wife

THE STORY

At one time, it was fashionable, in Melbourne, to have spent the years of childhood in a working-class inner suburb where everyone had a chook house down the yard.

Chook house nostalgia gripped the hearts, the hearts of all the barristers and of all the wives of all the barristers in Carlton. Long and narrow channels of their brains were furnished with rusting sheets of corrugated iron, lacy panels of chicken wire, pollard and bran and shell grit. White Leghorns and Rhode Island Reds tark-tark-tarked through their dreams. They began to collect large paintings by artists about to be famous. Poultry appeared in these paintings. Men who could be seen by day wearing jolly little wigs and crossing William Street, their black gowns flapping, sometimes catching at the knee, by night lay beneath Danish quilts on Japanese beds beside Indian rugs, gazing up at a few hints of stars through new curved skylights, thinking, every now and again, about the straw in the nests. There was the colour and shine and smell of the straw, and the gleaming hint of the china egg which they had hidden there to encourage the hens to lay.

The wives of these dreamers also gazed up through the skylights in the renovated terrace houses, as proud visions of the White Leghorn rooster, his long tail-feathers curving, his comb standing up like play-dough, strutted across the skylights of their minds. Mistresses, generally speaking, were spared these farm-yard scenes, for they were as a rule too young for chook house nostalgia. In fact, they were inclined to have been born in wealthy suburbs in times when Rhode Island Reds no longer tark-tarked at the bottoms of gardens, but lived, still and quiet with hundreds of their sisters, their beaks and legs useless, laying eggs for rich farmers. Those who had studied biology at the most expensive schools had, of course, been given an egg to hatch and a chicken to carry round under their pullovers, but there was no connection whatsoever with the farm-yard.

So by now you are beginning to imagine the kind of life led by Maureen (known, by the way, as Buffy) and Stanford Fox.

They were about forty, and were building up a collection (amongst all their other collections of wines and paintings and Limoges china) of books about the crisis of the middle years of mankind. No book in their collection made any reference to the important part which

the chook house of childhood plays
in the crises of the middle lives
of Carlton barristers and their wives.

Stan lay on his futon, underneath his doona, next to his dhurrie, thinking of money, and of Melanie, and of what it was like when he was four. All he had wanted for his birthday when he was four was a little black hen. He had got that hen, and her feathers glittered in the sun which shone all day every day when he was four. There he was in his tartan shirt and his khaki overalls.

In the books—*You and the Mid-life Adventure; Professional Man at the Crossroads; Births, Deaths, and The Ageing Process*—eminent psychologists explained that at any time after the age of thirty-five, Stan would probably grow "dis-enchanted" with the Law. Had he ever been enchanted, he wondered. The books went on to tell him that he would be seduced by any one of about four fantasies:

There would be the sailing-around-the-world fantasy, or the becoming-a-creative-artist fantasy, or the running-away-with-the-girl-from-the-milk-bar fantasy. Or the back-to-the-earth. The title of this last one worried Stan. He was about to be forty-one, and he was staring at the skylight and working on the back-to-the-chook-house fantasy which was not described in the books. It escaped Stan's notice that the back-to-the-chook-house was but a variation of back-to-the-earth. And that being in love with Melanie was the running-away-with-the-girl.

Carrillo Mean wrote of the function of nostalgia for childhood and the obsession with nursery foods. He dealt briefly with the phenomenon of back-to-the-school-room as a mis-direction sometimes taken by men in middle life when they seek, as Mean put it, "the authority of the dominant school-mistress figure". As noted earlier, it was going to be years before Mean would write *Buff Orpington and the Disasters of Middle Life* —a name adopted, incidentally, by a group of feathered singers. In fact, Mean would cite the case of Stanford Fox Q.C. in a detailed footnote to the third chapter.

Stan lay in bed planning to find a little place in the hills. There was a tall pine tree at the front, rather like an illustration in *The House at Pooh Corner*. Water babbled over nearby rocks.

Look, look, there are clumps of bluebells, and carpets of wild freesias in the spring. Rabbits peer from behind the stumps of trees. On green wicker chairs beneath an apple tree, sit Stan and Melanie. Melanie is wearing a sort of transparent nightgown that might have appeared in a film in the forties. Her hair, a mixture of cornsilk and soft ripples of amber with flashes of topaz, is long and ruffled. Her feet are bare in the dewy grass. They are drinking Russian caravan tea from dainty cups with violets painted on them. The cups belonged to Stan's grandmother. The teapot is blue and fat. It has a little chip in the spout, just where Stan's mother's teapot, also blue, had a chip. As Melanie gestures to emphasize a point, the Milk Arrowroot biscuit between her fingers is snatched away by one of the hens which fidget around her feet.

Buffy lay in bed and thought about the fountain which she planned to put in the courtyard in the middle of the house. She stared up through the skylight and thought about the Italian fountain, and about money, and the children, Bib and Bub, and about Tony.

Every Monday Buffy met Tony at the beach house. She had been doing this for five years and had seen Tony through his divorce from Barbara and his marriage to Margaret. If, as sometimes happened, Tony was unable to get to the beach house, she went there by herself. She would make avocado dip and lie on the old sofa reading Doris Lessing and listening to the sea. And still, after all this time, she had visions of Tony. She lay in bed in Carlton and Tony would float across the fashionable skylight. His outline would, it is true, occasionally recede as sharper apparitions of the two Italian boys from the bike shop pedalled into view. Buffy would imagine herself feeding imported chocolates into their open red mouths. She would buy the chocolates in little gold mesh bags from the coffee shop just down the street, and, dangling the bags from her fingers, she would stroll into the bike shop to buy a tail-light for Bub's bike. And there they would be, the boys, wiping the grease from their fingers with a grubby cloth.

As she lay in bed, Buffy decided that she would ring the plumber tomorrow. She would have the fountain in the central courtyard, the babble of its water echoing the sound of the stream on the country property blooming in Stan's head.

For Stan's birthday, they had a dinner party. Tony and Margaret were there. And so was Barbara, Tony's ex-wife who was married to the orthopedic surgeon who had put her bones together again after Tony had pushed her down the stairs.

"When I was four, I got a little black hen for my birthday. It was all I wanted. And I really loved it. I called it Natalie. I was madly in love with a girl called Natalie."

"We had about a dozen Buff Orpingtons at one time. When we

lived in Northcote next-door to the Italians that were supposed to have shot the man in the TAB. God, they were pretty little things. The chooks I mean. Like cornsilk with ripples of amber and flashes of topaz. In the sun."

"I was famous for my chook imitations. Tark-tark-tark-tark."

"But that's wrong. It's puck-puck-puck-puck."

"It is not. They go cluck. I know it sounds like something out of a school reader, but they really do go cluck. I know. We had about twenty fowls, and ducks as well, and the hens definitely said cluck and the ducks, believe it or not, said quack."

"French ducks say coin-coin. I've heard them. When we were in Brittany last year, Madame Thing kept the most fabulous ducks in the sort of basement part of the house. And they all said coin-coin. All the time. You could smell them in our bedroom, whatsmore. It was just above them you see."

"But really, don't chooks say a sort of mixture of tark and quick?"

"What sort of chooks did you have, that said that?"

"Well, Australorps. You know, little black hens. Tark-quick, they said. Always."

"Oh, Australorps."

"My sister took a photo of me with the little black hen, and she won a fountain pen in a photographic competition."

"Have you got the photo?"

"No. When I was about sixteen, I think I tore it up."

"Oh, what a pity. We could get a little Australorp though, and we could take some more pictures of you. And it. We might all win fountain pens."

"Buffy does a really good imitation of a rooster. Go on Buff."

"Cock-a-doodle-doo."

It was then that the discussion moved on to talk of the bouquets of the wines, and the effect on the middle palate. We may record that the Mouton Rothschild was really quite delicious, and everybody became rather drunk.

It was on a sunny day in spring that Buffy took Bib and Bub onto the bike path by the river. The children had yellow helmets with scarlet straps. Flags on tall stalks fluttered behind them as they rode. They looked rather like little soldiers in some modern and yet medieval war. The boys from the bike shop whizzed past on a bright red tandem, almost knocking Buffy from her bike. They waved, and kept going, shouting something cheerful in Italian.

On this same sunny day in spring, Stan and his sweet Melanie were inspecting a small property in the hills behind the city. A dusty pine tree grew by the front gate. There were bluebells in clumps by the tap at the back door. Water trickled over the pebbles of the stream which marked the northern boundary. And an asthmatic sheep-dog dozed in the dust.

That night, at Melanie's house, Stan had a heart attack. The books had warned of this.

They had been sipping Châteauneuf-du-Pape, and leafing through a poultry catalogue.

"Let's have one of everything," said Melanie, her hair a ripple of cornsilk, flash of amber, dash of topaz.

Buff Orpingtons, Rhode Island Reds, Australorps, White Leghorns pecked cheerfully at grain in the pictures in the catalogues.

"*The birds must be induced to take sufficient exercise in the house.* That would be their own house, wouldn't it?"

Stan drained his glass, smiled at Melanie, embraced her, caught his breath, and fell onto the peach velvet settee.

It was while Stan was in Intensive Care that Italian workmen came to install the fountain in Buffy's courtyard. Water gushed from it in a shiny cone that overflowed like a melting ice cream. In the sunlight, droplets of water winked like stars.

"Stan will find it soothing, won't he, watching the water and listening to it. When he comes home?"

Buffy was talking to Tony on the telephone.

"You've done a great job, Buff. Hold the phone up to the water again for a minute. It sounds great. Just great."

"Come round later," said Buffy, "I've just put the Veuve Cliquot on the ice. And you must see what I've bought for Stan. It's the sweetest little statue, just like Natalie, the hen he loved so much when he was four."

The Enlargement of Bethany

Harry Stone the optometrist stood behind the window of his shop. The window was frosted and on the outside was painted a large pair of golden spectacles. The lenses of these were of clear glass which Harry polished on both sides every morning so that the surfaces were as clean and sterile, Harry liked to think, as the human cornea. Harry was standing behind one of the lenses looking into the street. Plenty of people in the street were wearing spectacles, and most of these had been made by Harry. It was a small town. Harry was prosperous and knew the distance in centimetres between the corners of the eyes of most of the population of Woodpecker Point. He knew the state of their retinas and the names of their grandchildren. Prosperous also, and also knowledgeable, was the undertaker who had the shop next-door. His window too was frosted, bearing the words "Lawrence Usher—Undertaker", a simple statement of fact in ornate gold lettering. Here there were no lenses to be used as peepholes. Laurie Usher's son, Robert, was courting Lisa Harrison who was Harry's receptionist. Harry found it distasteful that Lisa and Robert sometimes went out to dances in Robert's father's hearse, but he said nothing as Laurie was a very old friend and Lisa was a fairly good receptionist. Harry was thinking about some of these things when he saw, through the lens of his window, Bethany Grey.

Every morning Bethany straightened and dusted the display
in the window of the Orchid Frock shop. This window was of clear
glass decorated at the top with graceful lozenges of green and gold
and an occasional amethyst disc. Between the bottom of the window and the pavement there were seven rows of shiny amber tiles.
This morning Bethany took the hats and wigs off the three plaster
dummies. Then she removed their arms with a clever twist, pulled
their dresses over their heads, and left them standing there smooth,
creamy-white, naked, armless while she hung up their dresses to be
ironed. Harry fancied a look of embarrassment crossed the dummies' faces as they stood in the window without their clothes looking into the street full of busy people wearing spectacles.

Bethany lived in the flat upstairs from the Orchid Frock shop.
She had wall-to-wall floral carpet on the stairs, in the hall, the bedroom, the lounge. The bathroom was black, black and shiny with
gold taps and a gilded mirror. Beside the mirror grew a dark pink
orchid in a black pot. She liked to lie in the black bath all covered
in bubbles and pretend she was glamorous and beautiful. She was
not. Harry knew none of these things about her or her house, but
he imagined some of them with reasonable accuracy.

"When he isn't testing people's eyes," said Lisa to Robert, "he
gets behind those glasses in the window and just waits for girls to go
past. Or else he watches Bethany Grey."

As Harry watched, scraps of transparent green paper fluttered
in the street against the tiles at the bottom of the window of the
Orchid Frock shop. The lonely naked dummies stared blankly into
space. The reflections of cars slid between them and the world.

"I am leaving to get married," said Lisa. "Robert and I are getting married in six weeks."

Bethany came back with three new dresses for the dummies.
These were silk ones, green like the cellophane which blew, ruffled
and crumpled in the street. She slipped the rippling silk over their
heads, down their bodies, placed their arms in the sleeves, adjusted
them in artistic poses, and stood back to admire them. She flicked
their skirts with her hand. She gave them fashionable wigs.

"Congratulations." Harry did not look at Lisa who sat behind a bowl of fresh flowers on his right. She was efficient, pretty, young, and in love with the son of the undertaker. Harry was in love with Bethany Grey who nearly always wore a white linen collar on her dress and didn't need glasses. Harry was waiting for the day when Bethany would step out of the Orchid Frock shop, look both ways before crossing the street (her shoes were nearly always navy blue, Italian) glance at the huge golden spectacles on the window, push open the door, smile at Lisa through the fresh flowers in the bowl and make an appointment.

"What did he say?" Harry asked Lisa.

"I beg yours?"

"What did he say when he asked you to marry him. He did ask you to marry him didn't he? Well what did he say?"

Mr Stone must be thirty-five and very experienced. He had travelled to London, Paris, Berlin, New York in search of spectacle frames in the latest styles. Whatever was he getting at? Why was he asking her this? She answered obediently.

"He said, 'I'm going into the firm. Do you want to get married?'"

"So what did you say?"

Harry Stone was still watching Bethany as she shifted the pieces of costume jewellery around the floor of her display window.

"I said—I can't remember what I said."

"You must have said yes."

"I suppose I must have."

"I am going into the firm. Do you want to get married?" He said it softly.

"I beg yours?" said Lisa.

"Nothing. Nothing, Lisa."

Bethany had gone from her window. The dummies stood in their artistic poses, their green silk dresses elegantly draped about their plaster bodies.

Then suddenly Bethany was standing (white collar, blue dress, navy shoes) in the doorway of the Orchid. The wind stirred the pieces of green paper in the street and ruffled Bethany's brown hair. She looked both ways and began to cross the road. Harry turned swiftly from the window and went into his consulting room.

On the wall was a chart which showed a colourful diagram of a cross-section of the human eye. There was a leather chair more comfortable than the one at the dentist's, and lights, screens, instruments, a reading chart, the satisfying perfume of darkness and science. It was all ready for Bethany to come in and settle into the chair saying, perhaps,

"I have been subject to mild headaches," or

"I can no longer see to thread a needle."

But of course she would be making her appointment. Lisa would be flicking the pages of the appointment book, running her fingernail down the times. Bethany would be looking from the parting in Lisa's blond hair to the petals of the chrysanthemums in the bowl to the ruled-off sections in the book. Perhaps there was a cancellation this afternoon. The Brigadier unable to make it. Suffering from gout.

"I have come," Bethany would be saying, "to make an appointment with Mr Stone."

"Would two-thirty suit?" Lisa would answer. "We have a cancellation."

Harry opened the door of the consulting room. He looked down at his shoes. There was rich brown carpet like furry chocolate on the floor. Silence. His shoes were black and shiny. For a moment he thought he should photograph them against the carpet. Some of his best subjects came to him like this in times of emotional stress. He caught the tail end of what Bethany was saying:

". . . be very happy."

It was an odd way to talk about an appointment, but perhaps she was as excited about it as he was. She had waited years before making the time. It must mean a lot to her. What sort of condition would her eyes be in? He looked down at his shoes again. He would bring the camera in tomorrow. A rustle and the thud of the front door. Bethany was gone. Harry emerged from the consulting room. Lisa, like some pale sweet angel, sat behind the gold chrysanthemums staring into space, a space occupied by her dreams of Robert Usher and the block of land they were buying out past the Bluff, not far from the old toy factory.

"We are going to build," said Lisa. But Harry was not listening. He was looking down at the appointment book. Looking for the name Bethany Grey, or B. Grey, or Miss B. Grey. There was a Black, a Miss Black.

"That," said Harry. "Who is that at 3:15?"

"A lady rang up. Said she was an old patient. I found her card. She's really old."

"Theodosia Black. I know. Never mind." Then he couldn't stop himself from saying, "What about Miss Grey?"

"Miss Grey?"

"Miss—er—Bethany Grey from the Orchid Frock shop. When is her appointment?"

"Oh no. She only came in to congratulate me. She was very sweet. She said she knew Robert when he was a baby. I didn't know she was a patient. She isn't a patient is she? She's going to do my dress. And the bridesmaids. I'm having two. Jenny and Ruth. Do you think they're too pretty? I don't want to be overshadowed."

"She didn't make an appointment."

"No. Can I have twenty minutes extra at lunch please, Mr Stone? I need to go to the Morning Glory to see about the cake. For the wedding."

During the afternoon of astigmatism, myopia and long sight, Harry began to recover from Bethany's rejection. By the time he went home to the Edwardian villa left to him by his late mother he was back to his old self. He thought he would offer to take the photographs at Lisa's wedding. Photography was his hobby.

Under the stairs at the back of the house he had built a dark room. He derived intense delight from seeing the images appear. The pictures he took of his shoes on the consulting room carpet were, however, rather disappointing.

Lisa's mother had for years nurtured a desire to engage a professional photographer for an occasion. So when Lisa and Robert announced their engagement one of the first things Mary Harrison thought of was booking Prism Studios, known for their artistic and flattering work.

"What would Harry Stone know about wedding photos anyway?" she said.

But Lisa assured her he would be very good, and said it was so sweet of him to offer. Mary moaned about it for a few days, then concentrated instead on the flowers and the music, the cake, the reception, the invitations, the bridesmaids' health, the cars, the hairdresser. There was plenty to do. She bought her own frock from the Orchid Frock shop. As it happened it was one of the green silk ones, and she bought new silver shoes.

Harry became alarmed when he was seated next to Bethany at the reception. He had very little conversation at the best of times.

"Call me Beth," she said. He couldn't. He seemed to be taking an incredible number of photographs. Mary Harrison was pleased and just hoped they were good. Through Harry's mind from time to time went Robert's fatal words to Lisa:

"I'm going into the firm. Do you want to get married?" He would try substituting other words to fit the circumstances:

"I am expanding the business. Do you want to get married? I'm going to buy a car. Do you want to come for a drive? I have some new frames from Paris. Do you need glasses?"

He finally dared to take two photos of Bethany. Hundreds of shots of Lisa and Robert. Two of Bethany. She looked rather serious.

Mary Harrison was delighted when she saw the wedding photos. The whole wedding party looked like princes and princesses. Would Harry mind doing a very large print to go over the lounge-room fireplace?

That was when he decided to enlarge one of the photos of Bethany. He would enlarge it and go over the road and give it to her. At last he had the words. He would say:

"I did this enlargement for you. Do you want to get married?"

No, he couldn't say the second part. But the first, he had the first. I did this enlargement for you. He could start calling her Beth. Perhaps. He wasn't really sure he wanted to marry her anyway. Did he really want her in his house all the time? Filling the bathroom up with tins of floral talcum powder.

It was a huge enlargement of Bethany. Harry looked into its eyes and then he saw them, the images. Reflected in each of Bethany's eyes were three little skulls, two upright, one reversed. Impossible. He was going mad. Somebody was playing tricks. He printed the photo again. He enlarged the other one. There they were in both pictures, six little death's heads, four up, two down. Like two little families in her eyes, the mother, the father, the upsidedown child. It was the Purkinje-Sanson Principle.

From his bookshelf he took a textbook and read:

> Whenever we seen an object, that object is reflected in each eye, not once, but three different times in three different places. This threefold reflection is caused by the curvature of the cornea. Two of the reflections are always right side up and one is always upsidedown. Depending on the angle at which the object is seen, the three reflections occur on different parts of the eye because of the differing angles of curvature of the cornea.

Did this help? Did this explain? Did every photograph of a human face contain six little skulls, three in each eye? Enlarge the image and the skulls would appear. Harry then looked into the empty eyes of Lisa and Robert and the other members of the wedding party.

It did not occur to him to destroy the enlargements. He stuck them on the wall of the dark room. He would know they were there but nobody would ever see them. He made a small print of one of them, and fancied that even then he could discern the skulls in Bethany's eyes. He felt compelled to give the photo to her. He thought:

"I did this photo for you. Do you want to get married? I think there is something the matter with your eyes."

He put the small print in a thick cream envelope and crossed the road. The dummies were naked, their arms in a heap on the floor, a vase of nasturtiums at their feet. A common sort of flower to have in a fashion display, thought Harry.

With a sort of flourish he gave the envelope to Bethany. She smiled as she thanked him and then she said:

"I have been meaning to come over. Make an appointment. I have been having a bit of trouble with my eyes."

Cherries
Jubilee

or
Whichever Way
You Look At It

Once upon a time
There were three babies—
Hamish, Martin, and Baby.
Hamish and Martin were born
with broken hearts;
Baby was born
with no brain.
It was a race between
Hamish and Martin
to get Baby's heart.
Hamish applied
to John White
for help.
Martin applied
to Organ Bank.
Hamish won.

John White has a beautiful smile. This smile is known to millions of people because John is the host of the most popular television chat show in the country. John is probably the most popular man in the country. The show is called Tonight With White, and comes on at eight o'clock with an orchestra playing the theme of the Brite'n'Wite toothpaste company which sponsors it. John has been appearing in advertisements for this toothpaste ever since he was six and actually had no front teeth. Even without teeth, he was adorable. His eyes are lovely too. He is forty now, and does not look a day over twenty-five. His private life is a complete mystery. He lives alone with servants and dogs in a mansion overlooking the bay, the golf course, the freeway, and an exclusive lawn-cemetery. On his program he interviews rock stars and their families, film directors, vice-chancellors, dustmen, politicians, prostitutes, professors, bishops, drug addicts, celebrated novelists, football heroes. And he also takes up causes which he and Brite'n'Wite consider to be worthy and newsworthy.

When Olive and Geoffrey McMillan's first child, Hamish, was born with hypo-plastic left-heart syndrome, the family was advised by their doctor to get on Tonight With White and appeal for a new heart for Hamish.

Marissa and Pablo Sanchez were watching Tonight With White. When they heard Olive and Geoffrey tell their story, they telephoned the Sacred Heart Medical Centre where their son, Baby, waited for death in his mysterious plastic and electronic world. Baby had been born brain-dead.

"We want to donate Baby's heart to Hamish McMillan," said Pablo. "If our Baby could help him, then it would not be a total loss."

So the spokeswoman for the Sacred Heart Medical Centre called Tonight With White, and every viewer in the country heard her say:

"We have a heart for Hamish."

Among the viewers were the parents of baby Martin Carpenter. They heard those words—*We have a heart for Hamish*—they saw Olive and Geoffrey collapse with emotion; they saw the studio audience go wild with joy; saw John White's smile of triumph and ecstasy; heard the theme for Brite'n'Wite toothpaste played loudly over and over. Baby Martin Carpenter suffered from hypoplastic left-heart syndrome. He was waiting in hospital for a heart to be donated. His doctor had placed his name on a list with an organ-procurement network. The Carpenters called their doctor, Rodney Barlow. He was watching Tonight With White and was rather expecting their call. Rodney then called Organ Bank, requesting a heart for Martin Carpenter. Organ Bank took three days to come up with an answer, and the answer was: WE HAVE NO AVAILABLE HEART. SUGGEST PUT CARPENTERS ON TONIGHT WITH WHITE.

But it was too soon, said John White, to feature another baby organ-transplant. Maybe in six months or so. This week his leading story, major theme, was teenage alcoholism. The country was seething with problems. One thing at a time.

Martin Carpenter died. A day before his death, as a last resort, Dr Barlow made a personal visit to the doctor in charge of Organ Bank.

"Yes, I'm sorry, Rod. It isn't easy. But as you are aware, you can't serve up hearts like Cherries Jubilee."*

Dr Barlow was aware of that. The doctor at Organ Bank went on:

"And when you put a heart in, I don't have to tell you, the road ahead isn't rosy. It's easy to put a heart in, but it's hard to keep it there. You could only get one whole baby out of those three, whichever way you look at it."

---

*CHERRIES JUBILEE
Simmer some fine, pitted cherries in syrup. Drain them. Put them into little silver dishes. Boil down the syrup in which they have been cooked, adding to it a little arrowroot diluted with cold water. Pour this liquid over the cherries.

Then add to each dish a tablespoon of warmed kirsch and set flame to it at the moment of serving.

Woodpecker Point

Named for the legendary Tasmanian woodpecker, which nests only on the northwest coast, the town of Woodpecker Point is the site of the first settlement in this part of the island, and is classified as an historic town. Many of the early buildings can still be seen, including the ruins of an imposing gateway which originally formed the entrance to a deer park. The most striking and most photographed feature of the rugged Bass Strait coastline at Woodpecker Point is the Blowhole, leading to which there is an easy walking-track. Excellent beaches, good fishing, and some of the finest agricultural land in Tasmania make Woodpecker Point one of the most interesting tourist centres on the coast. Of particular note are the hawthorn hedges so reminiscent of old England, and the tiny church of St Mary-in-the-Fields is as fine an example of the architectural traditions of Europe and Britain as the visitor could hope to see. Other attractions include the old Part and Parcel Inn, and the Den of Antiquity where locally collected period furniture can be bought.

Trekking Tasmania
C. Mean, Bedrock Press, 1985

RALPH GERMAINE PEACOCK, GARDENER AT THE MORNING GLORY
MANSION, WOODPECKER POINT, BEGINS THE STORY, AUGUST 1986

I like to think I am descended from Hugh Germaine who
named such Tasmanian towns as Bagdad and Jericho when he travelled about in the bush. We have much more than our name in common, Hugh and I, for, like him, I always carry a copy of the *Arabian
Nights* and a copy of the Bible. I have never felt the need for any
other books. In the evenings, when I have finished my work, I light
the fire in the cottage, have my supper, and read from each of my
books before tackling my real work, which is a collection of sermons I am writing.

I am called to live alone and to labour in the vineyard of the
Lord which I take to be, at this time, Alice Morning Glory's garden.
My sermons will be illustrated with photographs, and I have
recently been fortunate enough to purchase, for a very reasonable
price, a fairly new Nikon FG-20 that turned up at the local antique
shop. I have made a photographic study of the inhabitants of
Woodpecker Point as they go about their daily lives, and I will use
some of these pictures in my book. My great and perhaps unrealiza-
ble ambition is that people should listen to my sermons on cassette
and watch at the same time a continuous live television broadcast
of daily life in Woodpecker Point. The words would be timeless, but
the illustrations would change and develop from minute to minute,
from day to day, and would also be recorded. It would be like a full,
permanent, animated photograph album. It is stream of conscious-
ness television. The program, like the book, is called *The Eye of
God.* I want people to see the world as the Lord sees it, and to hear
the Lord's interpretation in my sermons, simultaneously.

"Thou God seest me," reads the text that hangs on my wall.
There are 387 references to the eye in the Bible.

And, "*Behold, I shew you a mystery; we shall not all sleep, but
we shall all be changed, in a moment, in the twinkling of an eye, at
the last trump: for the trumpet shall sound, and the dead shall be
raised incorruptible.*"

George Glory was killed in Egypt during the war, leaving Alice
a widow and childless. She has never recovered from that tragedy,

but has found consolation in the Gospel, and in her garden, and in the running of the Morning Glory cake shops, famous for miles around for Morning Glory fruit cake which they sell by the pound or by the slice. The recipe is no secret.

MORNING GLORY FRUIT CAKE

(domestic quantity)

8 oz. self-raising flour
4 oz. sugar
12 oz. mixed raisins, sultanas and currants
2 beaten eggs
4 oz. softened butter
¾ teaspoon mixed spice
scant ¼ pint milk
pinch of nutmeg
pinch of salt

Mix the flour with the sugar and dried fruit. Stir in the eggs and the butter. Add the milk and the spices. Beat all together until thoroughly mixed. Turn into a cake tin lined with greaseproof paper. Bake in slow oven for 2 hours.

1986—MURIEL PLUM RECALLS EVENTS FROM THE 1940s

I was standing with my twin sister Iris in the lane, clay and dandelions under our feet, blackberry bushes nearby. There would be snakes, or at least a blue-tongue living in the blackberries. And just behind the cowsheds there were pigeon-lofts, cooing, always cooing in the close distance. Crying pigeons with broken hearts from the glinting green of caverns hollow under sea behind the tormented dark of the blackberry bushes.

Mad Mick who milked the cows and was not dangerous but smelled of cowsheds was yodelling to the milkers. Keep them happy. They like music. They give more milk. And cream.

The cows are the colour of gillyflowers, soft as pansies, smelling like Mad Mick.

We stand under the cherry-plum tree, holding the yodel in our ears, holding in our hands the fairies we have made from shuttle-cocks covered with a down of purple thistle, fluffy with puffs of dandelion clocks.

It was evening then, and sun came slatted through the fence, drifted in spangles through the leaves of the cherry-plum.

Mrs Morning Glory lives at the top of the hill. Windy trees, dark and smelling of dust and cypress, cemetery and rosemary. Behind a white white wall, high as a convent, in that Spanish Mission house, pink as dolls' house ham, sits and eats and walks and sleeps; sews and laughs and talks on the telephone Mrs Morning Glory. She is so glorious. Her whole back fence is covered with morning glory. (A noxious weed of course you know, but she—the likes of her—thinks she can get away with anything and everything, and does and did. And take what you like and pay for it, says God, the great Comeuppance). And she wears, on some afternoons, a vast and spreading mushroom of a hat which is blue, morning glory blue.

There is a peacock gleam of sapphire in her eyes. A spark of garnet darting from her heart.

She looks at us, at me, at Iris. Who are we? Who could we possibly be, Iris and me, our ears full of sad pigeon-whispers sifted through the prickles of the blackberry bushes lurked in by blacksmiths and scarlet glittering snakes with eyes no sooner said than done.

But Mrs Morning Glory has no children. It is the tragedy.

She will not understand us. Will not think that we are here, standing at her fancy gate, iron, painted white with a bell like in a convent. She is a mystery to us. But you can imagine, can you just ever imagine! What a terrible puzzle, mystery, riddle, cowshed blackberry clackberry we are to her?

There we are, Iris and I, folded up in the sweet dark pink of Mother, top and tail, (Mrs Cherry Plum is having twins) waving to each other, little kicks and punches and an elbow in the stomach, swimming now and then and discussing the noises of the pigeons and the terrible blindness of the baby kangaroo. Then remember, Iris, how Mother split suddenly and we were dragged out to sea in the current, and the waves were pulling and pulling, and there was such thunder and firebird-danger-lightning, frightening with a dragging groaning earthquake uprooting, and we flew? I flew so suddenly into the splashing light, the cold air on my anemone old face, and you followed me at once for fear, I suppose, of getting left behind, getting stuck, shut in, lost, and even dead back in there in Mother, gasping for breath and crying, howling like the cow.

Mad Mick will yodel for you at the christening. I don't want that silly fool at the christening. Time enough to think of all that when we have severed the cords that connect the ties that bind. Two thick beating twisty cords like the cords of telephones, purple and shiny and slimy with words. Then, two kangaroos, we found our way to Mother's milk and she was sweeter than a cow, much, much sweeter than a cow. We cried. We cried and cried and cried so that Mrs Morning Glory could hear us at the top of the hill. There she sat on the blue velvet chair like a chair in a convent smelling of gold, smelling of gold, and also of frankincense, but most of all there was a smell of myrrh, so bitter and so sad, a smell of cypress and yew tree and rosemary and even lavender, but more of cemeteries.

I looked into the garden, and, just beyond the snowball tree, I saw the most beautiful thing. Tiny weeny little pink rosebuds. Buds there were, folded and darker like kisses in the centre. And open pink roses, open with curling feathers like chrysanthemums. The smell like strawberries and pepper and roses, pink and mysterious as incense in the dark. Iris used to wet the bed. I only did it once.

There we were, folded in the swinging swimming dark when Mother went walking in the lane, went to get the milk in the billy, up the lane, past the cowsheds among the dandelions and thistles and blackberries, listening to the weeping of the broken-hearted pigeons. Sobbing their hearts out. Mother walked past the high white wall, and when she looked through the gate she could see up the gravel drive, edged, you know, with the most fabulous polyanthus, bright as blood, and she could see Mrs Morning Glory at the doorway of the house which had been photographed many times for *Home Beautiful*, and written up in the *Weekly Times*—Spanish Mission, every luxury, black marble in the bathroom and a refrigerator with a maid in the scullery and Mr Glory dead in the war went off singing into the sunset over the hill, waving his rifle, the rising sun glinting on his hat so very new and khaki. (What an Urdu word that is.) He was wounded in the leg, a leg wound in the desert and could not get to water and he died of thirst in the dust like a fly—I think it must have been like a fly—in the desert. He looked like a currant, one wrinkled little currant on the surface of the cake of Egypt, a very old place to die.

He was a pastrycook in civilian life, owned half a dozen cake shops and always took the prizes at the Royal Show.

When Mother looked through the gate, and we were rocking nicely in the bag, Mrs Morning Glory was also roundly inhabited by her unborn son. But no, oh no! the dry and aching demon shock of the currant on the cake, the fly in the dust, caused a thin and smiling Turkish weapon, something like a scimitar—Oriental curved sword usually broadening towards a point, of unknown etymology (the French is "cimeterre"—ominous word)—to come slicing through poor little Mrs Morning Glory's heart and belly, and, eventually through her brain. The loss of her husband and the miscarriage of her baby, as we understand it, turned her mind.

Somehow she could never speak to Mother after that.

Mother wheeled us yodelling in a navy blue pram up and down the hill. Slow up, fast down. "This is a War Savings Street" it said on the notice on the electric light pole. And Father was away in the navy on the safe wet seas with all the water in the world to drink and Mr Glory was only a currant on the Egyptian cake. We were a terrible reminder of baby Georgie Glory (named after the king in defence of whom Mr. Glory had fallen in battle). He was minute, perfect, dead, the image of his father, baptized in a very sad ceremony, and buried in a hallowed section of the garden where later on the gardener and Mrs Morning Glory wept and planted an almond tree.

She could not see us. She looked right through us as though we were the ghosts or the yodelling mad.

"This garden," I said to Iris, "this garden looks like the garden of the Selfish Giant."

Mother was very clear that we were not to worry the poor

soul. She had everything that woman, everything that money could buy. She had, don't forget, a refrigerator. Stay away from there. But the other world beyond the convent wall was pale and sweet, the air filled with butterflies, the trees glowing with waxy lemons and red apples from the tree of Mrs Morning Glory's Knowledge. She was guarded by a dog and a gardener with a purple face. With a basket and scissors, wearing gloves and the blue organdy hat, she drifted around her garden, snipping and sniffing, and taking roses inside to arrange in the crystal bowls she was given as a wedding present.

I reached the iron curls of the gate, and cupped my hand warm wet living child hand around the pale green globe of the flower on the snowball tree. I tugged. The snowball came off the tree and lay full of green and white air in my palm, stray florets drifting onto the path.

I felt the shock of guilt dash wildly through my veins. We ran home down the lane past the pigeons and the blackberries and the cowsheds. The snowball was crushed to tatters in the hand of the thief.

The roar of the gardener's roaring wide-open mouth. "If I catch you I'll ram it down your bloody throat." The thin and jagged wail of Mrs Morning Glory's anguish swirled in tarantella through the sparks of all the stars.

> They have stolen my flowers.
> They have taken my glory.
> My baby will never come back.

THE MORNING-GLORY STORY

I lost the baby after I heard George had died. First he was missing, and then, they said he had perished in the desert. Like a piece of elastic. Perished. The news went through me, through my soul like fire. I knew the only thing left for me in the world was the baby. I prayed that it wasn't true about George. But it was. I prayed hardest of all for the baby. But he died of grief inside me.

That's what they said. He died inside me. I died inside. Lost inside me and nowhere left to look for him. George was dead in the big world desert, and the baby was lost inside me.

It was midnight. The telegram was under my pillow. I was lying in bed in the big bedroom at the corner of the house. You can look out of that room into the rockery, across the spikes of the lavender, across the tops of the fruit trees, and right out to sea. There was a distant sighing and moaning and the telegram was under my pillow. My thoughts kept swinging from George, so young and beautiful, his eyes like sunlight. I loved him. Kept swinging back and forth from George to the baby, rocking like a cradle back and forth, back and forth. And my tears rained like the sap from the bark of a wounded tree. I lay in bed, my head on the pillow, the telegram under the pillow, and I prayed for George and I prayed for the baby, and with my hands I caressed the baby inside me.

Then I felt fire darting hot and sharp through my body. A blob of blood slid out of me. I stopped crying. My hands were still. I was as still as a stone effigy in my bed of stone. The stars outside the window ceased to move. The moaning and the sighing of the waves was silenced. Then the hot blood gushed out of me into the bed and I lay there, perfectly still, my mind arrested with the stars and the waves.

For hours, all night, I lay there as life flowed away, and I was flowing with it, going with the baby, going out of life.

But in the morning someone came and found me. I went to the hospital and when I was just becoming conscious, I heard a voice saying,

"Yes, she lost the baby."

Lost. Lost. Where can I search for him? In my mind, in my heart, in my weeping soul, I searched for him. High on the tops of bright mountains where clouds of glittering butterflies drift over the rocks; deep, deep in the beds of streams gurgling with sparkling fish; far, far down in the rainbow caves of the secret earth where spirits glide and chant in low mysterious chorus—I sought him.

"Perhaps we had better let her see him then," said the doctor. "Perhaps that would be best."

They brought him to me, cold and perfect, pale as a pearl. He was wrapped up in a white lace shawl. He was the smallest doll. For some reason, I had not expected him to be naked. I sat up in the hospital bed with the baby in my arms, and I turned back the shawl. His legs were folded up, his wrists crossed under his chin. The tiny globe of his head. The kiss of his lips. I kissed his lips, afraid he would dissolve. And he was naked. His toes were like buds of orange blossom, and like the Christ Child in the painting, he was naked on his shawl. Made from flesh and curled up on his shawl.

Sometimes I can't believe all that has happened. It is a long time ago now, and yet it still is as clear and sharp as now.

And the child was naked.

Somebody came to visit me in the hospital. They brought flowers, and a paper bag full of mushrooms. I left the mushrooms under the bed. I have never forgotten them.

MURIEL WRITES TO IRIS

Woodpecker Point   October 1986

My dearest Iris,

The mosquitoes are terrible this year, but still Father will not let me fill in the old well. I truly believe they breed in there. He is dying. All day long he sits in his chair with Auntie Ann's red rug on his knees, and stares out to sea. Out past the old palm trees, over the rocks, and far, far out across the water. As though he were still hoping to see Caroline and Arthur come floating back. He has no fingernails. They sort of dissolved as his illness got worse. And his hair is as white as a baby's, thin, and standing up on end. I rub the citronella on his face and hands as he sits out there in the dusk, staring out across the ocean, portraits of Caroline and Arthur mirrored in his eyes. The mosquitoes do not bite him and his beautiful eyes have faded. They are now the tinge on the edge of a glass of buttermilk.

You will come home for Christmas, won't you Iris. And we will go and look down again, down, down from the purple pig-face, down, down the sloping cliff into the suck suck suck of the blowhole. Arthur and Caroline, happy young tragedy rolling slow at first and then faster faster down the slope of the pig-face into the mysterious pounding darkness of the blowhole frilled with froth.

Auntie Ann said that Caroline would be the death of Arthur. Well, who knows? We would rub the citronella on our arms and legs and go out for walks at dusk to pick the flowers poking through the fences of people having tea. Through the windows we could see the pink frilly flounces on their tablecloths, and there was cucumber green as toads, little green toady frogs that live down the well. Always one jump ahead, and we never caught a toad. But we came back with our arms full of somebody else's snapdragons and petunias, and we sat under the palm trees to suck the nectar. Out on the rampage raiding people's gardens. The stuff in the middle of petunias is poisonous. People have died. Father sitting dying in the cane chair in the garden not far from where I found the egg.

I parted the leaves of the violets thick with darkness and velvet mystery, and pearly in the heart of them was an egg. I was quite used to handling delicate things, and I picked it up with ease, and let it rest in the palm of my hand while I stroked it very gently and whispered. There was no shell, but a soft membrane dusted with pale pink powder, gently beating like the top of a baby's skull.

You will come home now, won't you Iris my darling, now that Father is dying, and I am all alone, small and alone, my darling Iris, in the dark.

Your affectionate sister,
Muriel

MURIEL WRITES TO IRIS

Woodpecker Point   November 1986

My dearest Iris,

Crêpe paper always reminds me of poppy petals. The red especially. Poppies, all kinds of poppies, but above all the red ones, are Father's favourite flowers. I have planted dozens of them in the bed along the front fence. He will be able to see them, bright between him and the sea.

Today I tidied out the bottom of Mother's wardrobe, and there I found the old basket, the one with coloured flowers on the side. I used to love those fat pink hollyhocks, but they are faded now. Anyway, in the basket I found a bundle of crêpe paper party hats we used to make with pointy edges just like clowns. They were scattered with old bits of lavender like the droppings of mysterious mice. And there was a red hat. It was the colour of the birds I used to dream about. Oh no, I used to say, they are not the colour of our blood at all, and they are not the colour of goldfish. No, they are the colour of tree-blood, these tree-blood birds that flick and skim through the veins and arteries of the forests of my night. And crêpe paper, as I said, always reminds me of poppy petals.

The red hat which I found in Mother's basket wasn't just the texture of a poppy, but the exact same colour as well. It was the hat, I remember, that Brian wore. You remember Brian, don't you? He came to all our parties in the garden. Every year until we were seven and he was eight, and he hanged himself from the branch behind his father's shed. We have never talked about this, Iris. But as I go through Mother's things, so much unsaid comes back to me, and I wish that you were here and we could sit under the palm trees where we used to put the table for the parties. We could talk about the things that we remember. If you do come for Christmas, my darling Iris, we will look at Mother's things together and compare our memories.

I remember Brian's face. It was always full of pain. I used to stare at him when I thought he wasn't looking, and wonder why he screwed his eyes up, why he squinted at the light, and smiled as if he really wanted to cry. He didn't want that poppy red crown at all. But Mother said oh do come on Brian it will suit you perfectly and her fingers caught a little on the roughness of the paper. He looked more sad than ever then, the red crown slightly crooked on his forehead. He was so blonde and used to burn so quickly in the sun.

It was our birthday, Iris. We were seven that year, and there were silk flags on the cake. I loved those little flags, Union Jacks and Australian flags. I must search for them among Mother's things. They always looked so important standing up between the candles on the cake. It's a wonder they didn't ever catch fire. I never really liked Brian at all. But when he just went down the garden and hanged himself from the apple tree with the belt of his father's pants, I felt a most peculiar rush of love for him, or a great sadness for life, or a terror at the ease with which he had crossed the line between life and death. Without making a sound. That was what his mother told our mother. He did it without making a sound. Noiseless dying on the branch of the apple tree. I imagined him dangling there with the red crown on his head, the tips of toes in his grey socks (I hated his socks) just grazing the top of the long grass. It's still there, you know, the tree. The fruit were never anything special, and now they are very sour little things. They ought to think about cutting it down.

I used to hope that Brian was a ghost who would speak to us, but he never did. And nobody ever talked about him, did they? It was as if he had never existed. He wasn't a ghost, and he wasn't even supposed to be a memory. I wondered what his mother did with his train set and his teddy. He had a Noah's Ark too. In the little photo of our seventh birthday party, there he is sitting on the piano stool next to his sister Jennifer, squinting into the sun, his head on one side, the paper crown all crooked.

Then in the photo of our eighth birthday, Brian isn't there, and Jennifer is sitting alone on the piano stool as if she didn't miss him at all. And the hats are all the same, and the flags on the cake are the same. And I seem to think that in the corner of the picture I can see a bit of the apple tree. But that is all there is of Brian.

If you can come home for Christmas, my dear Iris, we shall go through all the photograph albums. There are so many things to remember. And there are also the albums full of pressed flowers and ferns. The petals of the poppies are as thin as dreams; the tulips shine like sinews. I burnt the paper hats. I think it was because the red one brought back to me the sight of Brian squinting at the sun, and I was flooded with an unbearable sadness.

Your loving sister,
Muriel

JENNIFER WRITES TO MURIEL

Woodpecker Point East   November 1986

Dear Muriel,

I hope that you remember me from ever so long ago. We used

to live next door to you when we were children. I remember you and Iris and Arthur, how we collected shells and starfish, and how we used to play in the hedge. Well I have just recently come back here to live, and I have been looking up all my old friends. It would be so nice to see you. I heard that your mother had passed on and that you were there looking after your father. I have never forgotten your mother's big wardrobe and how we used to dress up in her things and put on her shoes and go marching off up the street. And once we all got into terrible trouble for leaving your father's red blanket out in the rain. There are so many good times to remember. When I have settled in over here, I must come round and see you and we can talk about old times.

> With best wishes,
> Jennifer Lilley

AUNTIE ANN WRITES TO MOTHER

Hobart   April 1945

My dear Margaret,

I am longing to come and see your dear baby Arthur. In the picture you sent he looks exactly like Iris and Muriel at his age. How are they? I have almost finished the blue dresses I was knitting for them. I did the two-year-old size. So I hope they haven't grown too much.

The red rug is coming along very well. I have sewn together all the squares I have knitted, and I am very pleased with all the different shades of red that we have found. Could you, do you think, send me ten more skeins, and then I will have enough to finish the whole rug, and you will have it in time for Christmas. You know how slow I am, and I do seem to let other bits and pieces get in the way. Won't James be surprised! It will be the first thing I have ever knitted for him since the scarf I did when we were ten and I had just learnt to knit. You should have seen it. It was full of holes and he hid it in the bottom of the wardrobe.

I am doing a bonnet for Arthur. I'll send same with the dresses for the girls.

Hope you are keeping well, and Arthur is sleeping.
With love,
         Ann

MURIEL WRITES TO IRIS

Woodpecker Point   December 1986

My dearest Iris,
         Today I found something that was so wonderful it seemed
almost miraculous. You remember the red birds of my dreams. Well
you must also remember I used to speak of a bright red windmill
which turned and turned in a perpetual wind above an endless field
of yellow wheat. And the sound it made as it turned was what I used
to describe as red laughter and it was so deep and soft and menacing
and sinister, that laugh. Mother would say it was just a dream, it has
no meaning and it is nothing to be afraid of, there is nothing to be
afraid of. And then I used to cry and say that there really was a
windmill, and that out beyond the field of wheat there was a sea of
tulips. Mother would say there that proves it, the windmill is just
something in a dream, there is no such thing as a sea of tulips. Well,
as I said, today I found something that was wonderful. I found a little
fluted dish and in the centre of it was a picture of the red windmill.
It was real after all. Of course I always knew it was real. And there
in the bottom of Mother's wardrobe, I really found it. It was wrapped
in tissue paper, and made from quite fine china, splashed with
blurred and iridescent rainbows. I was so happy when I found it, Iris,
but there was nobody to tell. Father was sitting in his chair, staring
across the water, gazing into his dreams. It seemed to be an impos-
sibility to rush out there with the windmill and explain about the
past and the dream and the windmill and the truth. But I did look
out to sea, and I saw again the sea of tulips, bobbing in the distant
purple breeze.
         I was standing right next to Father. We were both looking out
past everything, and then the red laugh started. Iris, it was coming
from Father. The windmill was turning in our father's throat, and he
was softly gurgling with the deep sinister sound. It was always like
a distant noise from inside the earth. Father sat there in his cane

chair, Auntie Ann's red rug across his knees, and I knew that the windmill was real, and Father was real, and the laughter of the windmill bubbled round and round in Father's throat. The miracle of finding the windmill had become once more the terror of the laugh. And now I have the windmill, and I have Father laughing, and I wish all over again that we could put back the dreams.

It will all be better, Iris, if you can come home for Christmas. Do say you will.

Your loving sister,
Muriel

MURIEL WRITES TO JENNIFER

Woodpecker Point   December 1986

Dear Jennifer,

I was so pleased to hear from you after all these years. You may have heard, since you wrote to me, of the death of my father. It was a peaceful end.

It is rather strange and touching that you should have mentioned the red rug. Father's sister, Ann, knitted it for him years ago when Arthur was a baby, and in the last months of life, Father could not be parted from it. He was always so close to Auntie Ann, and she died so mysteriously and tragically. Father used to sit in our front garden and stare out to sea, always with the red rug on his knees. When he died I had the red rug buried with him. I know he would have wanted that, and it seemed the correct thing to do.

So now I am living in the old home all by myself. Iris is still in Portugal and I have so far been unable to get in touch with her. It is so sad. She would have wanted so much to see Father again before he died, and now he is gone.

I found some photographs with you in them. You must come round soon and have a look at them and we will have a talk about days gone by.

With love,
Muriel

MURIEL WRITES TO IRIS

Woodpecker Point   December 1986

Dear, dearest Iris,

    I have tried so hard these last few weeks to get in touch with you, to find you out there somewhere in the world so far away. I have stood on top of the cliff and I have fancied that I saw you on the dark green rim of the horizon as I wept. For Father has died. I went out in the evening with his cocoa as he sat in his chair in the garden, and he was as still as a toy, our small toy father in his favourite chair where he died.

    I needed you to be here, my darling Iris, to help me and to tell me what to do. There was a stranger passing on the street, and I called out to him.

    "Please telephone the doctor for me," I called. It seemed to be the right thing. The stranger was only Brigadier MacArthur, and he stayed with me until the doctor came. He was so kind. I missed you so much Iris. All I could hear was the croaking of the frogs down the well and the slow and terrible roar of the terrible ocean snarling in from far across the world spurting up the blowhole and sucking back our souls.

    There was one of those summer storms on the day of the funeral, and all I seem to remember is the sight of so many umbrellas at the cemetery black and navy blue and the organist's orange hat in the church. We had chrysanthemums. Some of them were pink. Afterwards, when the storm was over, I walked along the beach.

    Home is very big now. I walk around it and wonder how we ever filled it. There were over a hundred people here the day Arthur and Caroline got engaged. That was the last time, wasn't it, that we had people here. The day after that was the day they were lost. And Father is gone now, Iris, and now that I have tidied out Mother's wardrobe, I have decided to sell the bedroom suite. The Brigadier is a dealer in antiques, and says he can guarantee us a very good price. Do you remember Jennifer Lilley? Well she brought me a basket of oranges.

Christmas has come and gone, my darling Iris. Do you think that you will get home soon? The poppies are just coming out now.

Your loving sister,

Muriel

FATHER WRITES TO MURIEL

Part and Parcel Hotel   January 1987

Dear Muriel,

I know how much you like to get a letter, and so I thought I would write as soon as I got here. I am not sure about stamps and so forth, but if I give it to the girl at the desk and give her a nice smile, she will post it for me. It was comforting to find a Part and Parcel here. As you know, the old Part and Parcel in Brisbane Street was always a favourite haunt of mine.

Well imagine my surprise when I got here and found that George Glory had been living here for years. I am sorry to say that he has not aged well, and has become a very boring old fellow, far too fond of the bottle for his own good. I bought him a double brandy for old time's sake, but from now on I will be avoiding that corner of the bar. He said he has never been back to see Alice since she lost the baby. I said I thought he ought to go occasionally, or at least drop her a line. But he said that the way she carried on with the gardener was more than he could bear. I said I had never heard of any such thing, and he just gulped his drink and snorted in a most unbecoming fashion. He also said that the cake shops have gone completely to the pack, but I can't see that at all. Wouldn't you say that Morning Glory's in Elizabeth Street was immaculate? I spoke of my preference for Dolly Varden cake, and I fancy he deliberately blew smoke in my face. His manners really have gone down hill.

Speaking of smoking reminds me that I would like you to send me some Navy Cut if you would. I can't seem to get it here. Otherwise I have everything I need. Thank you for packing the red rug. Even though it is getting rather threadbare, it is still quite cosy. The poor fellow next to me got the most awful chill.

So far I have been unable to locate your Mother and Ann.

George said he didn't think they were here, but I wouldn't really be prepared to trust his memory these days. Really, Muriel, he is pretty well shot to pieces. I am also trying to get in touch with some of the fellows from the ship. I believe they drink at the Mermaid Tavern, but my taxi-driver yesterday refused to go there for fear of getting beaten up. Said it is in a very unsavoury part of town.

I met some people who have recently been in Portugal. I plan to ask them if they heard anything of Iris. It's just a long shot, but you never know. Won't learn anything if you don't ask.

I am writing this in the lounge, looking out across a sort of caravan park with the sea in the distance. The golf course is somewhere over to the left, and there are apparently some good walks. Masses of rhododendrons.

Somehow or other I managed to forget my camera and binoculars. I think they must be in the bottom of Mother's old wardrobe. Would you mind looking them out and sending them to me?

I'd like to put together a set of photographs of this place. As far as I know, it hasn't been done before, and I was just getting used to my new Nikon.

I am your loving Father

IRIS WRITES TO MURIEL

Portugal   January 1987

Dear Muriel,

Your letters were waiting for me when I came back from the Pyrenees where I have been on holiday for the past six weeks.

I am so dreadfully sad that Father has gone and I did not see him. It seems he did not suffer, and I know you cared for him with great devotion.

There was something I thought of. As a small memento of Father, I should like to have the red rug Auntie Ann knitted. Do you think you could send it to me as you tidy up? I would be so grateful.

It would remind me of Father, and also Auntie Ann and Mother and Arthur. I was trying to remember, the other day, what Caroline's surname was. Do you know it? I fancied, when you said MacArthur, that it was that, but I am just not sure.

I think it is wise to sell some of the big furniture, and you probably ought to get the well filled in.

Your loving sister,
Iris

MRS MORNING GLORY'S ANECDOTE, MARCH 1987

Mr Sailor Cherry Plum Pip has died and gone to heaven. They dressed the admirable admiral up like a sailor doll, and put him in a box with his lifesaver. Just like the man who stares from the packet of Navy Cut tobacco, all white ropes and a beard. Mr Sailor had blue eyes too, and a naval funeral with a white rope umbilical cord and full navel belly-button honours and a guard of honour like a game of lead soldiers.

That man wished to be buried at sea. I have seen him sitting in his garden, staring out at the water, chuckling brightly into the Prayer Book. Man that is born of a woman hath but a short time to live. And we therefore commit his body to the deep to be turned into corruption looking for the resurrection of the body when the sea shall give up her dead.

They buried him in the ground with his wife, the late Mrs Sarah Bernhardt Cherry Plum, and his sister Gorgeous Angelina, sister-in-law of Sarah Bernhardt.

"Oh how I wish," said Sarah Bernhardt to herself as she slit the belly of the barracuda, "how I wish that Gorgeous Ann would choke to death on one of the bones of this very large fish caught by my husband this morning."

If wishes were fishes there were dishes of wishes on Sarah Bernhardt's kitchen table. Mr Sailor went out in his great big motor boat with his sister Angelina, and hooks baited with practically the best rump, and caught a ton of slippery shiny gleaming silver barracuda silver fish.

"I wish that woman would choke to death on a fishbone wishbone," said Sarah Bernhardt.

And there they all were at the dining-room table, Mr Sailor Cherry Plum Pip sunburnt and glowing, Mrs Sarah Bernhardt who had curled her hair for the occasion, the twins, Iris and Muriel, (Arthur had not been long drowned, and had probably fed the barracuda), and Gorgeous Ann in a skimpy lace dress. They had silver dishes and dozens of double damask dinner napkins and Waterford crystal and with one great giant fish-bone Sarah felled her rival, Gorgeous Ann. Mr Sailor thumped his sister on the back as she went purple in the face, and he poured whiskey from the tantalus down her throat.

Her cheeks were covered with splashing waves of Irish whiskey from the best cut crystal. The whiskey mingled with her tears and trickled across her gorgeous breasts. She died in her brother's arms at the dinner table, as Sarah and Iris and Muriel stood at their seats, their mouths open in horror and alarm, their knives and forks clattering to the floor with accidental death.

Mr Sailor wanted to be buried at sea with all the other sailors he used to know, leaving Sarah and Gorgeous in their beds beneath the cypresses of St Mary's churchyard. I had afternoon tea with them all once. Earl Grey tasting like blue cheese and some very insulting little cakes which were iced in pink with a cherry on the top, exactly like little breasts. I know that Sarah made them with the help of the thieving twins who were looking like nothing on earth at the time. Gorgeous never did anything much except the obvious, and the occasional piece of very peculiar knitting.

So now they are all up there with head-stones. James Plum. Husband of the aboves. St Mary's church grows from the surrounding fields, and in the spring there are daffodils, planted a hundred years ago, like yellow figments of the imagination. It is a lonely Christmas card ancient church built by the early settlers who have settled well and truly into the earth, and the Vicar is keen to keep the churchyard beautiful for visitors who go winding up the track to it like medieval pilgrims. They read the head-stones of the Cherry Plum Stones. Little do they know of what is meant by all those marble words.

PICNIC AT WOODPECKER POINT—AS RECOLLECTED BY FLORENCE, SISTER OF BRIGADIER MACARTHUR

It was like an afternoon in Australian literature. Still air, bright sun, and a promise of tragedy. I don't think that's just hindsight. My niece Caroline was drowned on the picnic in 1965. She was engaged to the Plum boy, Arthur. He was all in white, with brown sandals, and she had a pale lemon frock with a gorgeous green sash. My sister, that's her mother, Gwendoline, was a beautiful dressmaker, and Caroline always had the loveliest clothes ever since she was a baby. They looked a picture, Caroline and Arthur. So young and happy. He was going to be an accountant. They found one of the sandals afterwards. It was washed up on the beach at Penguin. But they never found Caroline and Arthur.

Mind you, I didn't go to the picnic. The Brigadier and I always open the Den of Antiquity on Saturday afternoons. In those days we were the only antique shop in Woodpecker Point. It's a different story nowadays of course with the tourists. And the migrants, but especially the tourists. We had such a lovely Royal Doulton dinner service come in the day before, and I was putting it in the window when Caroline and Arthur walked past on their way to the picnic. They stopped and waved to me in the window, and Caroline looked at the plates as I was arranging them. I could see that she really liked the dinner service, and I thought at the time that if it didn't sell I might give it to her for a wedding present. Ironic that. As it happened anyway Mr and Mrs Lilley bought it the week after for Jennifer. She was getting married and I got a very good price for it.

Caroline had a picnic basket with the thermos sticking out. Funny the things you remember. And Arthur was carrying a tartan rug. A few minutes later the others came past. There were Iris and Muriel in floral frocks with white collars and big hats. I have a frock very like those ones in the shop at the moment. It came in a deceased estate just the other day. I should say it had hardly been worn. James and Margaret Plum and James's sister Ann went past, James ever the handsome sailor and Ann in bright orange towelling with those gipsy earrings and a striped umbrella. I really don't know how Margaret put up with her. She never lifted a finger in the house. Margaret had to do everything. And the girls, Iris and Muriel, were completely useless in those days. Couldn't boil an egg as they say. I remember one time I went up there to have a look at a crystal decanter they were getting rid of. It was supposed to be Waterford crystal. Waterford my eye. And the girls were making paper flowers while their mother was slaving in the kitchen.

Well they all went down the street and up the path that leads to the top of the cliff. And somehow in the middle of the afternoon, in the middle of the picnic, when the seagulls are hanging around the bits of rainbow cake, and the chicken and lettuce sandwiches are all gone, Iris is bitten by a bull-ant and Caroline and Arthur go for a walk.

The next thing I know, I've just got the Royal Doulton looking right and the Brigadier comes running in to ring the police or the ambulance or whatever. He had just gone down the road on his way to the Part and Parcel when Iris came screaming up to him out of the middle of nowhere in hysterics. Somebody had seen Caroline staring down into that terrible blowhole up there, and she just seemed to go forward, they said afterwards, and tip onto the side of the cliff. It's all covered in pig-face. And Arthur screamed and reached for her and they slid and rolled down the cliff and disappeared into the water. Sucked into the black blowhole and simply never seen again. I said how they found the sandal at Penguin, didn't I.

ITEM FROM THE PARISH PAPER, ST MARY-IN-THE-FIELDS,
JANUARY 1965

Memorial Service

On Thursday afternoon there was a memorial service in the parish church for Caroline MacArthur and Arthur Plum whose lives were lost when they fell from the clifftop at Woodpecker Point. The lesson was read by Mr Ronald Hope, and Brigadier MacArthur delivered the oration. Miss Ginger Hope played the Brahms Lullaby on the violin.

We extend to the families of these young people our deepest sympathy.

May light perpetual shine upon them.
The trumpet shall sound, and the dead shall
be raised incorruptible.

CAROLINE'S JOURNAL, JANUARY 1965

I love you.
Dearest Arthur,
I love you.
With all my heart.
I love you.
If I practice saying this, thinking this, writing this, it must come true.

I dream of you night and day because you are my one true love, my sweetest, dearest, only Arthur.

I love you.

I have decided to keep a journal because I think it will help me to sort things out. Sort out my life, my feelings. As I write "I love you" over and over like this, it begins to sound less true. It might have been almost true when I wrote it at the top of the page, but now I have worn it out.

I am not used to telling people I love them. Do I love them? Do I really love anybody? What does it mean? Mother? Father? Jane? Peter? Do I love Arthur? Will I love Arthur? Will loving Arthur come true like getting teeth or wrinkles or dying. I nearly died from pain and weeping when the vet said Toby would have to go. I must have loved Toby, and so I will try to remember how it felt. Then I can imagine loving Arthur.

I love you.
Arthur.

Toby knew I loved him. I didn't have to tell. Does Arthur know I feel nothing? No, it isn't nothing. But it seems to me it isn't much. Is it enough? Is this how everybody feels when they are going to get married? Love, honour, and obey. I don't believe I understand the meaning of "honour". And obey. What about obey? If he commands me to do something very awful, will I obey him? Do the words in the service actually mean anything? I do not obey, do not honour, do not love. "Obey" is the only one out of the three words that I understand. And I'm not going to do it.

Dearest Arthur,

I love you with all my heart and soul, my own true angel. I honour you and I obey you. I go to Ralph's cottage at the bottom of Mrs Morning Glory's garden. Ralph is the gardener. It is such a sweet cottage with ivy creeping all over the chimney. I wonder it isn't too hot for it there. He lives all by himself in the cottage with his Bible and his fishing lines and his rifles. His bed is really old-fashioned, a black iron one, and he has a quilt made by his mother. He always folds the quilt back before we get up on the bed. It is quite a high bed like in a hospital. Ralph is extemely tidy and likes me to put my shoes exactly side by side on the hearth. He is very particular and he is very religious. He thinks the Vicar is too high church, but he says his wife is a pretty good cook. She made him a bright yellow cake for his birthday. He was thirty. Seems old when you think of it. Mrs Morning Glory gave him a cup and saucer with violets on. I thought it was a little peculiar, giving a thing like that to a man, but Ralph was pleased. Sometimes he is not easy to fathom. He never drinks tea, and certainly not coffee. So the cup and saucer just sit up there on the mantelpiece next to the text: "Thou God seest me".

He puts pins and buttons in the cup and his late father's glass eye. Of course he is against alcohol and tobacco. He chews American chewing gum which he says is made by Christians in Pennsylvania. If I am very good, we eat Turkish Delight which he calls Rahat-Loukoum. And he is a good gardener, I know. He has made all the difference to Mrs Morning Glory's garden. I wish I understood how it is she loves her dead husband. He was killed in the war. Dear Mr Glory, I love you. With all my heart and soul and strength. Dear Arthur, this is just a note to say how much I love you. How much I love you. Deep down. I am deeply fond of you. Nobody ever says "deeply fond". Except Ron.

Dear Diary,

I am telling you everything in the hope that you will understand and help me. I think that I should somehow feel something for Arthur if I am going to marry him. He is so suitable. He is so sweet. Sweet Arthur. Dearest, sweetest Arthur, you are so very, very sweet, and I love you with every part of me. I am so deeply fond.

Ron is Ginger Hope's father. I went to school with Ginger but she's younger than me. She is clever and pretty and I will long remember with affection.

(Dear Arthur, I will long remember with affection the times we spent walking on the cliff.) The day when Ginger took me home with her for afternoon tea. I was so surprised when her mother said "Call me Audrey". And when Ron said "Call me Ron" I nearly fell off the deck chair onto the grass. Audrey was so perfect pouring tea from an enormous silver pot into the thinnest china cups you ever saw. The air around her seemed to tinkle. She was like a lady in a play or in a painting. That was how I saw her at the time. They seemed to be so happy. Ginger was turning cartwheels on the grass.

"But Caroline," said Ron, "is too ladylike to kick up her heels like Ginger." I didn't know what to say. Afterwards he drove me home. First we went to the top of the cliff and looked out across the grey and endless dreadful waves.

"You look like a mermaid, but I suspect you are not," he said as he put both hands, quite suddenly, under my skirt. It got late and dark and Ron was deeply fond of me.

I thought of calling off the wedding. Then I thought that was a bit melodramatic. Giving back the ring, sending back the presents. Cancelling the dressmaker and the reception and the church and the florist and the man who is tinting the satin shoes for the brides-maids. And the photographer. Telling the printer to unprint the invitations and the order of service. But now this thing has happened and I'm going to have a baby. So now I really do have to marry Arthur. I wish in a way that it was Arthur's baby. Failing that I wish I could persuade him to go to bed with me. That is what is really worrying me. But perhaps it will work out.

ARTHUR'S RECOLLECTIONS, JANUARY 1965

We always had to wash our hands before we played the piano and so it was a shock to me when Ginger Hope ate a large ripe peach and while she was still sucking the bits of flesh from the ridges of the stone she stretched out her fingers that were slippery with juice and started to play "Blue Moon". She had a gold bangle that slid up and down her arm while she played, and a little blob of peach-flesh came off her finger and stuck on a black key way up in the treble.

That day was the first time I had actually spoken to Ginger. She is younger than me and known as a child prodigy and her father is a poultry farmer so our families don't mix. In fact I never took much notice of Ginger. When she was playing the piano I was waiting for Mr Hope to bring Caroline back from a choir practice. Mrs Hope was sitting in the fernery reading her book and eating the chocolates I had brought. I was glad she liked the chocolates, but I was a bit surprised when she just took them and went out and sat in the fernery and started to eat them without even offering one to me and Ginger. She didn't care about Ginger and the peach and the piano either. Then Ginger said she was sick of waiting for her father and Caroline and she suggested we could go for a walk.

"Bring your camera with you," she said. So we went up the road till we came to the toy factory and then we went towards the cliffs. Ginger was talking a lot of the time. She said she was glad she was going to be Caroline's bridesmaid but she hoped there would be time before the wedding for her to have a new gold filling in her front tooth. I said you could hardly notice. Then she told me how her tooth got chipped in the first place.

"We were in Spain," she said, "and Mother who is, as you know, rather high church, insisted upon visiting every mouldy old shrine and creepy statue you could think of. We were in Segovia which is actually quite pretty, and Mother dragged us off to see the tomb of St John of the Cross. You have simply never seen anything so hideous and bleak as the Carmelite convent in Segovia. I shudder to think of it. Then in the church there is a grave, an actual hole in the floor where St John of the Cross was first buried. He must have been no bigger than a dog then if that's true. But next to the hole there's this huge tomb where they put him later. It's all lapis lazuli and bronze. I was so tired and bored and worn out anyhow, and the place honestly smelt like an attic full of dead dogs, that I sort of tripped and bashed my face on the lapis lazuli and that's how my tooth got chipped. I had a black eye and you should have seen the blood.

"*En una noche oscura,*
con ansias en amores inflamada.*

. . . I don't know the rest."

"It doesn't show," I said. "The chip I mean." But Ginger said she's very self-conscious about it.

We had reached one of the little hollows high up in the rocks where you can sit in the shelter of a kind of cave and look right out across Bass Strait. I have never been out of Tasmania myself and Ginger's talk of Spain was very exciting and sophisticated.

"You brought the camera didn't you," she said. And then she asked me to take some pictures of her.

"Pretend you are an explorer and I'm an aborigine," said Ginger, "and you've never seen anything like me, and you take pictures of me for a learned journal and become famous."

Then she took off her clothes really fast and stood with her back to me, sliding her bangle slowly up and down her arm, looking out across the water. When she turned around she was laughing and her skin was as white as sugar, tight across her bones, and there were freckles on her arms and a tuft like russet seaweed between her legs. She made me take nearly the whole film of her and then she said, "Now you take off your clothes and come over here."

She made me do it. I didn't really want to. I had never done it before. She frightened me. I kept remembering Caroline. There was sweat glistening on Ginger's temples where her coppery ringlets trailed damp and flat. She looked beautiful but somehow horrible too. Then she said, "Now take another photo, thorn in the flesh, fly in the ointment, nigger in the woodpile."

I couldn't understand her, but I was suddenly very angry. I pulled the film out of the camera and chucked it into the sea. It glinted as it flew out and twisted and curled, down down until it hit the water far far away beneath us.

"Stupid," said Ginger.

> *Owing to the inefficiency of the postal service,*
> *this letter was never delivered.*

Upon a gloomy night,/With all my cares to loving ardours flushed./St John of the Cross Translation by Roy Campbell, Penguin Classics, 1960

Oasis Caravan Park   February 1965

Dear Mother and Father,

    This letter is very difficult for me to write. I know that it will come as a great shock to you to learn that I have decided to begin a new life here.

    A number of extremely sad things have happened to me in the past few weeks, and I find it would be impossible for me to return home, in view of these things.

    I hope that you will both forgive me, and will come to understand my position and my feelings.

    I must reassure you that I am well and safe, and I am applying for the job of assistant caretaker at the caravan park which is quite busy at this time of the year.

    I will write to you again when I am more settled, and in the meantime I hope to hear from you.

    I am your devoted and loving son,
        Arthur Plum

P.S. The photograph of Caroline and me that was taken at the Prism Studios must be destroyed. Please do not ask me why, but I am quite firm about this.

FATHER'S MEMORIES OF ARTHUR, JANUARY 1987

    I was out walking today when I passed the Oasis Caravan Park, and I recalled a dream I once had about poor Arthur. He had taken a job at a place of that name. Seeing it like that brought back all the sadness and longing for the boy, brought back the feeling of emptiness I experienced for so many years after his disappearance. I think the greatest disappointment in my life was that I never had a grandchild, that when Iris and Muriel pass away there will be no more Plums. If only Arthur and that dear girl Caroline had lived and had a little family. And Arthur was doing so well.

MURIEL REMEMBERS HER FATHER'S FUNERAL, JANUARY 1987

    I keep trying to write a letter to Iris, to tell her what happened to the rug, but the words will not come any more. Pieces of the day Father was buried come back to me, and I think I should tell Iris more about the funeral, but the words float away, dissolving before they get onto the paper. There were lots of people there. I want to say, and it was raining. They came hurrying up the path through the fields, dark mushrooms of umbrellas bobbing between the stone fences. Was it the rain or was I weeping all the time? Something was ticking in my head, and all the brasses and the coloured glass in the church were blurred, uneven, shifting and shimmering in the smell of old hymn books and mould. I love that smell. We had a very old aunt who smelt like that. Great-aunt really. It was far far away from the sound of the sea. There was no sound inside the church. The thick stone walls have stopped sound. Outside, the rain, the wind in the pine trees. Inside, the closed granite silence filled with giant puffs of white and pink chrysanthemums and suddenly the scarlet orange wail of the woman at the organ. Was it "Jesu Joy of Man's Desiring" in my blurred and rainbow ears? A rustling and thumping of people and umbrellas. Oh the wet world bloomed with the chrysanthemums of human voices. And Father lying quietly, shut in the small dark silence of his coffin lined with silk. He was dressed up in his handsome uniform, and then I covered him with the rug, just like putting him to bed, the sailor in the little brown bed in the dolls' house lined with silk. He was as quiet as a mouse, as good as gold, and they all praised the Lord with songs. And flags and dust. In the doorway of the church, standing in the porch, there was a piper. His legs were like trees, knobbed with knuckled knees and his kilt was misty with the dyes of ancient battles green and scarlet, his face like an inflated plum sending the air of blessing, the breath of god and the brightest red of all the reds was the tassel swinging on the pipes. I stood right next to him and people stared at me, so out of place, and I traced with the fingers of my eye yet blurred with spray, the arabesques carved into the silver rings on the pipes. Then he seemed to stand forever at the graveside in the rain under the pine trees, piping at the graveside, piping Father out out out across the water bobbing in his coffin on the waves, nice and cosy in his rug and lined with silk.

I stared at the crack in the wall of the church, high up like a spider getting bigger every year.

The Vicar shook my hand and said again that Father was a

good man and would be missed. All over the floor of the church, there were puddles from the umbrellas. And then we had hot scones and tea at the vicarage with Mrs Blake-Showers, the Vicar's wife, with a new pink carpet since the Vicar is new. Mr William Blake-Showers and his wife. She kissed me on the cheek and he shook me by the hand. The piper was sitting in the corner of the room, his face and his pipes quite silent and deflated. I fancied that he had fallen asleep. The grey sky wet between the curtains fitted into the window like a tile. Oh I was unhappy then.

THE REVEREND WILLIAM BLAKE-SHOWERS SPEAKS TO DR DE SAXE, THE G.P., MARCH 1987

I have been very worried about Miss Plum ever since her father passed away. She has always been a bit eccentric, but I became really alarmed when I called on her one afternoon not long after the funeral and found her sticking plastic poppies into the flower-bed along the fence. It is not good for her to be there in that big house all by herself. Her only companion in the evenings is the television, and I believe that it over-stimulates her.

She came round to the vicarage yesterday practically in ecstasy and told me that her father had made a special guest appearance on her television in the middle of the weather. She said that he said he had written to her asking her to send him his camera which was in the wardrobe. Her problem was that she sold the wardrobe to Brigadier MacArthur from the Den of Antiquity and didn't clear it out properly before she let him take it.

Well I rang the Brigadier there and then, just to humour her, and he said that all he found in the wardrobe was an old parcel containing a baby's bonnet and two little knitted dresses which he put on a doll and a teddy bear in the window of the shop. Miss Plum said he was welcome to the baby clothes, but I do believe that she suspected him of having stolen the camera.

It is only natural for a single woman of her years, I suppose, suffering as she is from the recent loss of her father who meant the world to her, to have episodes of paranoia. Not to mention the hallucination during the weather.

I know that you have attended the family for some years,

Robert, and wondered whether there was some way you could have a word with her, and perhaps form an opinion. I strongly suspect that she will require a course of treatment from a specialist. But I leave such decisions in your capable hands.

THE G.P. REPLIES, MARCH 1987

Well, I was passing the Cherry Plums' at lunch-time, and there was Muriel out the front weeding the flower-bed by the fence.

I admired the poppies and so forth, and was regaled with the information that the best blooms were Rhode Island Reds, and the more fragile ones were Silver Campines or Golden Pencilled Hamburg Hens. I think perhaps her condition is harmless enough. She doesn't appear to be at all depressed, and spoke very warmly of the Brigadier. I'll keep the notion of psychiatric intervention up my sleeve for the time being, but I honestly don't believe that now is the time to uproot her from her home.

Thank you for bringing the matter to my attention, however, and I shall keep an eye on her and see that she doesn't get any worse. Incidentally, she's not really as old as she seems. Perhaps April could drop in on her occasionally during the course of her parish rounds. It would seem quite natural for the Vicar's wife to call, and you might tell April that Muriel makes a very acceptable egg-and-bacon pie. Or used to.

FATHER WRITES TO MURIEL

Part and Parcel Hotel   March 1987

Dear Muriel,

It was a great pleasure to be able to speak to you. I chose to do it during the weather because I knew you wouldn't want me interrupting your programs. I thought you were looking a little pale. No sign of the camera here as yet. The post in this area is apparently notorious for being unreliable. George says he has written dozens of letters to Alice, and sent her boxes of Turkish Delight every birthday, but has never heard a word from her. He thinks this means the post is tampered with. Of course, I generally take what he says with

more or less a grain of salt. The poor fellow seems to be raving most
of the time.

I mean to tell you I have located your mother. She is staying
at the Chook and Cherry which is the epitome of old-world luxury
at the fashionable end of the main street. It reminded me of Brown's
in London. Remember when we all stayed at Brown's and you lost
your tam-o'shanter. Or was that Iris? Yes, well your mother suggested that I move into the Chook and Cherry, but I am really quite
settled here at the Part and Parcel. They do a very nice pumpkin
soup. You realize this place is all hotels. It seems that Ann is actually
running one of them, the Ali Baba next-door to the Mermaid
Tavern. I still haven't got into that part of town. Mother sends her
love, by the way.

Someone I did see though—and I know this will interest you—
was Nell and Ernie Blue's baby, the one who died in his sleep. He
has apparently become a Roman Catholic of all things, and lives
(also in great luxury) at the Prague. There is a group of nuns living
there, and they do very elaborate embroidery and dressmaking.
Boy Blue's mother would be astounded to see the kind of get-ups
they've had him in. I've seen him in the park feeding the ducks and
wearing a long brocade dress like an oriental prince. He seems quite
happy. I made a little yacht for him from a walnut shell and he was
tickled pink. You might pass that on to Nell and Ernie if you happen
to run across them.

If you are thinking of sending a tuck-box in the near future,
could I ask you to pack a Dolly Varden and one of your egg-and-
bacon pies. I really miss them, and you will be pleased to know that
I have a very good appetite at the moment.

I'll try to come and see you again soon during the weather,
although it isn't always possible to get through, and sometimes
there is a very long queue.

Your loving Father

MURIEL RAMBLES ON, APRIL 1987

Jennifer Lilley came again, with grey curly hair and twinkly
spectacles, carrying a basket of scones she had made. They tasted
like shoe-polish, and her shoes were dirty. I know in my silent self

that I have never liked Jennifer, never liked her at all. She always had fat legs and a mean mouth and I think she has never stopped talking in her whole life. Her husband ran off and left her. I didn't know that before. The wonder is that he ever married her in the first place. But people do. Mrs Blake-Showers suggested Jennifer was lonely, suggested we might be friends, suggested I was lonely. I am not lonely enough to have Jennifer Lilley around here all the time trampling over my flower-beds in her large and dirty shoes, plonking her handbag on the sofa. I am sorry now that I asked her to look at the photograph albums. She sat at the dining-room table running her index finger across the photos. When her finger came to Brian, it did not even hesitate, just went sailing across him, sliding on, flicking to the next page. "And you and Iris as alike as two peas. You always had such beautiful smocked frocks. I envied your smocked frocks." Her marquisite watch going twinkle twinkle tick tick tock, and a little silver chain dangling from it, tickling her fat wrist. "And you used to tell us stories about all the fairies you had seen. You had a wonderful imagination. Looking under damp leaves to find little processions. You described a wedding and how the orchestra was playing very softly under the chestnut tree. I half believed you."

I remember that little wedding and the sweetness of the perfume which filled the garden, and the delicate notes of the fairy flutes and violins.

And then when we were twenty-one, Iris went to London and never ever came back. I don't think Iris is ever going to come back now. I think she is living in Portugal with a Roman Catholic priest. That's what I think has happened. I think she went to art school in London, thousands of miles from Woodpecker Point, and went to Paris and had an exhibition, and went to Portugal. And in the light and the music and the flowers by the sea with the fishing boats, Iris fell in love with an aristocratic Portuguese priest in black with holy hands and shining pirate's teeth. Oh Iris is happy in Portugal.

One day the gardener from Mrs Morning Glory's came to the gate with a box of acorns.

"These are for the pigs," he said. And I said, "But we haven't got any pigs." He insisted. "My name is Peacock," he said, "and

these are for your pigs. Mrs Glory told me to bring them down here
for the pigs."

I walked away from him but he followed me. He followed me
across the garden and we went into the shed. He put the box of
acorns on the bench and we were standing by the window looking
out and looking in, when he took my face in his hands and kissed
me the way gardeners kiss and undid all the buttons of my dress.

"Hang this dress on the door," he said. "We don't want to get
it dirty."

And like the empty skin of a disappearing snake, my grey and
yellow-bellied dress hung from a rusty nail. We did those things
standing up. I didn't know you could do that. He left the box of
acorns behind, and I hoped he would come back to get them
another time, but he never did.

Father keeps telling me he has written to me, but I haven't had
any mail. He says to pack him a tuck-box at least, even if I can't find
the camera. I wondered how best to send the tuck-box, and then it
came to me of course. So I went down to the well to see how big the
parcel ought to be. It is a big well, isn't it.

It is a silent blowhole, still and black and sweet with slime and
mystery. There is a wonderful country down there with tree after
tree of apple tree, scarlet with fruit and Brian after Brian silently
swinging from a branch of every tree. His socks brush the feathers
of the golden wheat. A breeze ruffles by. A pigeon, broken-hearted,
is sobbing faintly, faintly sobbing in the hedge.

I packed the Dolly Varden, all chocolate icing and layers of
yellow and brown cake with currants dotted in the sand and mud.
And a very special egg-and-bacon pie just the way he likes it. I lined
the box with dried figs and dates, and wrapped everything in vine-
leaves and oil-cloth. It was a wonderful parcel. I tied a rope around
it and lowered it into the well.

First I walked around the well three times at sunset as we
always used to do. Down down down it went into the shining darkness of the watery earth. I took care not to bump the sides of the
well. I heard the parcel hit the water and felt it glide down until it
was swiftly pulled by swiftly-pulling forces. Fingers untied the rope
from the parcel. Oh Father will be pleased.

A WORD FROM FATHER, APRIL 1987

Muriel came good with the tuck-box. Just what I needed. I even shared the cake with George. That should show him that the cake shops are in good shape. He still complained that there weren't enough currants. The thing that pleased me most of all was that the parcel actually got through. There's hope for the camera and binoculars yet. Muriel certainly knows how to pack a parcel.

THE VICAR SPEAKS AGAIN TO THE G.P., APRIL 1987

Well, Robert, it is always possible, after the event, to see how a tragedy could have been averted. I suppose somebody should have realized that the Plums' old well had never been sealed off in any way. It is hardly my place or yours to go poking around people's gardens to see what's safe and what isn't. However, I shall certainly bring the matter up at the next Council Meeting, and would appreciate your support.

It seems that Muriel was dangling a pair of binoculars down the well in the semi-darkness when Jennifer Lilley discovered her and attempted to intervene. Before Muriel knew what had happened, Jennifer had toppled over into the well. Muriel ran for help, and as luck would have it, the Brigadier was passing on his evening walk. But of course it was too late. The poor woman had drowned. Miss Plum will certainly be needing medical attention at this stage. It is so terrible that this should have happened in her garden so soon after her own father's passing. Sometimes people's lives seem to be filled with sadness and trouble.

MRS MORNING GLORY HAS THE LAST WORD, APRIL 1987

A fresh flock of green and topaz spirits came flying up from the well when that woman drowned in it. They spread out across the sky above the cliff-top, streaming into the sunset-yellow clouds. Buttercups were blooming in the clouds above the cliff-top, washed with the brightest shining light which shines under the chins of children, do you like butter? Let me see now, do you like butter? And you held the yellow flower under the child's chin, and the sweet butter-yellow light shone up and the child was laughing in the sun. He likes butter.

I suppose that now the interfering Council will come with rumbling cartloads of cement and pour it down the well, the dangerous yawning drowning ringing singing buttercup shining well. Oh where will they nest then, the airy spirits of the air? Where will they nest and rest and whisper to the dead, whisper the secrets of the living and the dead.

I waved to them as they went by that evening. I was standing in the garden, breathing deeply of the sea air as the shadows of the evening were about to fall. From the corner of my eye, I could see as through a prism, the world in waves of splashing split light spilling. And at times like that, the sadness of it all, the drowning and the coroner and the sadness of it all comes rolling back to me and tolls like bells across the water, and drums with drums beneath the sea.

One man, my George Glory in his uniform of glory goes to glory in the desert and his throat is parched with thirst. But this woman in her tweed skirt with her wood-and-leather buttons topples headlong into the water down down down she hits the water, dreams her life away, and drowns. Shuts her eyes in astonishment as her glasses are whisked off by the well-water, opens her mouth, takes a deep draught through mouth and nose, and, suddenly there is insufficient oxygen in her blood, and brain and heart stop working. The end. The green wet slimy swirling glugging end. Oh, Jennifer Lilley has drowned now in Muriel Cherry Plum's dangerous garden well. The water of it all! If there had been some moderation, give and take and moderation, she could have shared some of that water. Could have had some desert; given George some of the water. He gets cooler; she gets warmer. He gets some peace; she gets some war. Baby Georgy Porgy Pudding and Glory gets into the water-supply and rides off on his hobby-horse around the ruins of the deer park. He looks so absolutely gorgeous in his red velvet suit with his golden curls and laughing hyacinth eyes. What a beautiful child, laughing in the sunlight, riding through the imposing gateway of the park, empty park where the wild gorse blooms yellow and prickly, where the ghosts of peacocks, the feathers of pheasants, the cries of the long-lost deer mourn the dead, the dear parched dead.

And Jennifer Lilley sinks like a dreadful rock in water, too much water.

Now lovely warm lights twinkle in the windows of the houses on the hillsides of Woodpecker Point. I have pink and yellow lights, and a cosy fire crackling in the grate. Down the lane at the Cherry Plums' house there are lanterns like beacons beckoning sailors, warning mermaids, flashing starry signals of distress. Votive lamps flicker in the grottoes of the Vicar. And his wife is rolling biscuits for the fête. Doctor de Saxe lives in a house like a giant snowball which glitters with glamorous health, crisp with white nurses and dazzling receptionists who called the ambulance which arrived too late for the revival of Jennifer Lilley. Big long strips of light like flags and ribbons deck the Council Chambers where the Council is discussing how much concrete you would need to fill the well. Supposing it is bottomless. Goes on forever, End-of-the-Earth well, dug by prehistoric insects which are still busy with the digging, their primitive little shovels forever going pick pick dig dig beat beat, little heartbeats in the pit of all the everything, and we hear those heart-beats faint as feathers, sweet as heathers in the heathery, feathery mist.

The Hair
and the Teeth

People broke into the house one time when we were out at the supermarket. I suppose we were gone for about an hour and a half. The older children were at school, but I had the two little ones with me. They were only three and two when this happened, and so whatever we did, we did it fairly slowly.

You drive to the shopping centre and park the car in the basement. Then you take the children out of their car seats and get to the lift that takes you up to the level where the supermarket is. You have to get the children past the toyshop with the Humphrey Bear that will sing and dance if you put money in the slot, past the pink elephant ride, past the Coke machine. If you put the children in the trolley at the supermarket there won't be enough room for the stuff you have to get, but if you don't put them in the trolley you have to be prepared to move very, very slowly. So you move slowly. You get the music, the lights, the smell of disinfectant, and all the colours. Everything shimmers in the supermarket.

(I find the music and the lights and so on very tiring and I am inclined to be irritable.)

You fill up the trolley and stand in the queue. The queue moves very slowly. Every trolley in front of you has things in it that need to have their prices checked. The music shifts from the Ascot Gavotte to the Easter Parade, and you cannot be soothed. You want to just grab the children and leave the full trolley where it is. But you wait and you pay and you wheel the trolley to the lift, to the car. You pack the car, strap the children in, park the trolley, drive to the exit, pay to get out, drive home. It is dusk now. When you get home you put your key in the back door but the door won't open because the burglars (What is the correct word here? Is it robber, intruder, thief, crook, bugger?) the burglars have bolted it from the inside.

As soon as the door would not open, I knew pretty well what had happened. I left the children and the shopping in the car and went round to the front of the house. The window was wide open and the curtain was flapping, in fact billowing out, like a miserable bride or a cheerful ghost. One of the children in the car had started to cry. I went back to the car, took two packets of biscuits from the shopping and gave a packet to each child.

"You can eat these," I said, tearing open the packets and handing them to the children. The crying stopped and both children looked a bit surprised but they obeyed. I locked them in the car and went round to the front door. This door has no bolt: I opened it, put my hand in to turn on the light, and stood for a few moments listening, and looking into the hallway. On the floor at the foot of the stairs was an earring, and halfway between the stairs and the front door was the lid of a jewellery box. The phone is on a table near the front door. I rang the police.

People tell me it takes a long time for the police to come to a break-in, break-ins being so common and policemen so rare, but these police seemed to be there by the time I had put down the phone. Possibly, because of the shock of the whole business, my sense of time was distorted. Anyway, the huge (it seemed to be huge) white car with blue writing and blue lights zoomed up the street and slid (really) in beside the curb and two police, a man and a woman, jumped (true) out and were suddenly standing beside me. The first thing I thought about was how healthy they looked. They looked just very, very healthy. He was big and young and smiling and sweet. And she was little and young and smiling and sweet. They had hats. They looked very clean—in blue, sky blue and navy. They both smelt of nice soap.

They searched the house for hidden people while I got first the shopping then the children from the car. The children had finished the biscuits. I gave them some chips. By this time the ice cream was beginning to melt and blood was dripping out of a plastic bag in which there was a chicken.

"Can you leave the kids with a neighbour while we get on with things?" asked the policeman. So I took them in next-door. Luckily someone was home and the children were were quite happy to stay there watching television.

We went all over the house, the police and I, finding evidence of what they said was the "work of a real professional." We sat at the kitchen table and made a list of what was missing.

I used to keep jewellery in the top left-hand drawer of a cedar chest of drawers. They must have emptied the drawer onto the bed-spread and then rolled up the bedspread and used it as a sack. I imagine two rat-like little men, real professionals, wearing masks, tiptoeing swiftly down the stairs, one with the sack over his shoulder, the other with an armful of leather coats. I start giving the policeman a list of things that have been taken: coral necklace, princess ring. He writes it all down carefully. The kitchen light seems to be too harsh, the paper the man is writing on too white. The clean strong police faces seem sympathetic but as helpless as the babies we have sent next-door. I offer them biscuits and coffee but they say no. Jade ring, silver bracelet with lapis lazuli. They have stolen a basket of firewood. The police cannot explain this. Suddenly I remember that among the sentimental treasures in the drawer were the locks of hair and the baby teeth of the older children.Then my voice starts to waver and I think I am going to cry.

(I had wrapped the teeth in a piece of silk and put them in a tin from a machine in the Paris Metro. Snow was falling. The Metro was warm. I put the money in the machine and got an oval tin of lollies with a wreath of violets on the lid. The lollies inside the tin rattled. They were dusted with sugar.)

Will I tell the police about the teeth and hair? Will I say in my litany:

"Two tortoise shell combs (Spanish), four ivory bangles (African), nine deciduous teeth (human), and two locks of human hair (golden)?"

They look at me kindly as I sit weeping at the kitchen table. I drink coffee and whisky. They keep writing. Periwinkle necklace, gipsy keeper (garnet).

I ask whether they think I will get any of the things back and they say that in a case of this nature, it is unlikely we will recover any of the missing items.

I put in the insurance claim and a woman from the insurance company came to interview me. She had a briefcase under her arm and a shrewd look in her eye. She was a bit fat but graceful with a black dress and a fur jacket and beauty parlour make-up, hairdo and fingernails. She was wearing Chanel, and her shoes were Italian. She stood on the doormat with the blue sky behind her and she could have been an advertisement for something, probably wine or, now I come to think of it, insurance. Or funerals.

"Mrs Halliwell from Phoenix. I rang," she said and I took her into the sitting room. You couldn't discuss the basket of firewood and the jewellery in the bedspread with Mrs Halliwell in the kitchen. I offered her coffee but she didn't want it either. The ordinary rules of hospitality do not apply to the police or to women from the insurance company. She had a typed list of all the things that were stolen. As she sat down, the sofa suddenly looked very shabby. A plastic fire-engine lay just near Mrs Halliwell's left foot.

"I will need more detailed descriptions of some of the items reported missing," she said, looking up at me over her glasses. "You will have to be more specific. A princess ring means nothing to me. What is a princess ring?" We came to the coral necklace which I said was made from round beads of coral, pale pink and smooth.

"Polished?" said Mrs Halliwell.

I said I supposed they were polished. "Angel skin," she wrote without speaking. Then she asked how long the necklace was, and when I told her she wrote "Opera length." Satisfied, she then said aloud, "Opera length polished angel skin," and she almost smiled. "Is there any other item you have omitted to report missing? This is your final opportunity to claim." I tried to think of something, as if I needed to please her. Then I thought of saying half the things I had just told her were lies. Then I remembered the hair and the teeth, and all I said at last was no. She said we would have to put

in an alarm system, arrange for security patrol, get security doors
and windows, or else get a reliable watchdog. I asked her for the
name of somebody who puts in security doors and windows, but she
said I would have to look in the Yellow Pages. Then she said "reliable watchdog" again as she tucked her briefcase under her arm. I
showed her out.

"And a peephole and a security phone on the door," she said
as she walked away.

The next day a man came to measure the doors and windows
for bars. He handed me his card at the door. On the card was a picture of a shark behind wire mesh.

"Jack McClaren," he said, "from Shark." He looked around the
garden.

"Nice large block. Surprising in this postal district," he said.
When he had finished measuring, and we had discussed the quality
of the optional one-way mesh and the need for the tri-safe locking
system with the three-point deadlocking and anti-pick lock, he had
a cup of coffee in the kitchen. We had some shortbread and a cigarette and I told him about the robbery. He said I was lucky and told
me about people who had been completely cleaned out. "Nothing
left standing except the electric light," he said. "Lucky you weren't
here when they came. Then they'd have done it with violence.
There's a terrible lot of armed robbery with violence these days. It's
on the increase. I see all the statistics."

So then I told him about the hair and the teeth, and he said that
was the worst.

"And the mongrels would just chuck those precious things
away, you know. I went to a lady's place who had all these photos
of her son from the war and they just let them blow away in the
street. In the rain."

As he talked I remembered something else that must have
been in the drawer. It was a small wax doll. I saw her one night in
the lighted window of a shop in the Palais Royale. She was a naked
little girl with blue glass eyes and a wig made from real hair. I went
back the next day when the shop was open. I thought she was very
expensive, but I bought her.

In the Conservatory

Once upon a time, there was a lady. She wore surgical boots. She lived in a house with a conservatory, and the floor of the conservatory was made of marble. Paved with squares of black and white marble. The lady walked on the marble floor of the conservatory with her surgical boots. Clop, stump she went on the black and white check floor of the conservatory. Marble. She carried a brass can, a little tiny watering can. She carried it into the conservatory and sprinkled water on the plants. Clop, stump, pitter, patter. She went surgical booting around the conservatory and poured fine rain from her watering can onto the soil. Onto the leaves. Pitter.

The sex life of the plants in the conservatory is such that it does not require bees. Bees, those messengers from the underworld, are not needed here. There are no bees in the conservatory. Life here is all a matter of the water and the spores. Ferns and light and dark and the water, pitter patter and the spores.

Yes, once upon a time there was a lady, and she wore surgical boots. Now this lady had two sisters. The sisters were called Sissy and Mags. Sissy was short for Cecilia, and Mags was Margaret. The original sister, the one in the conservatory watering the ferns, fish fern, maidenhair, was Alexandra. Named after the queen, the beau-

tiful one. So Ally was in the conservatory, watering. Sissy was tall
and she was dusting the piano. One of her eyes was glass. Sissy had
a little glass eye. Is that hard to take, after the news about Ally's surgical boots? Well, it is true. And what is also true, but *very* difficult
to believe, in the face of Ally's boots and Sissy's eye, is that Sissy also
wore surgical boots, and so did Mags. There was something funda-
mentally wrong with the family's feet. Apparently.

When Ally was in the conservatory, and Sissy was in the parlour dusting the piano, Mags was in the kitchen. She was cooking.
What was she cooking, then? Mags was making cauliflower cheese.
You could smell it all over the house. Practically. Cauliflower cheese
to go with the Sunday roast. Mags was in the kitchen in her beret,
cooking. She always wore the beret. Did she wear it to bed?
Probably not. But she wore it up to the shop, and always in the
kitchen, and in the garden, she was the weeder. Mags was the
weeder. She could be seen in the afternoons on her knees on the
gravel path, weeding the shrubbery and the flower beds. Her old
head in her old beret, bent in concentration over the weeds. The
beret was burgundy. Dark burgundy. Mags wore a dark burgundy
beret.

Out in the garden, there were bees. No bees, you remember,
in the conservatory. Yet out in the garden, there were bees. Yes,
humming furry messengers from the underworld. Messengers with
fine glassy wings veined with mysterious designs, honeycombed
with fine dark veins. Veins like the stems of the maidenhair fern.
Fragile, glassy wings of maidenhair on bees. The pattern on their
wings is the same as the pattern in the glass on the roof of the conservatory. The bees love this garden because it is full of lavender.
If the old ladies don't want the bees, they had better get rid of the
lavender. But they don't know that. Bees love blue flowers.

This garden is full of lavender and delphiniums and jacaranda
and wistaria. Amongst all the flowers in this garden, the blue ones
are the main attraction for the bees.

You will notice that we have slid into the present tense. The
blue flowers are the main attraction for the bees.

The aunts are wearing their boots. Ally, Sissy, and Mags. Great aunts in great boots, black boots. Laces crisscrossed on old ankles. There are three great aunts. Ally, Sissy, and Mags, and they have little crippled ankles, all of them. What, all of them? Yes, all of them. Little crippled ankles in little leather bootie boots, like black leather boots, crinkled on their ankles, little boots.

Ally carries a brass watering can. She waters the ferns in the conservatory where there is a black and white marble floor. Sissy has a duster and a pot of polish. Lavender and beeswax. True. She is polishing the piano in the parlour. The piano is an upright Steinway in dark wood. Behind the fretwork there is pleated satin. The satin behind the fretwork is red. Dark red. Sissy, with her one glass eye and her surgical boots, is polishing the piano. It has a lovely tone. It is an upright Steinway. Mags is in the kitchen cooking cauliflower cheese. She is wearing her beret (burgundy) and she is making the cauliflower cheese to go with the wing rib and the tomato pie and the mint peas. And gravy.

It is Sunday, and there will be a roast.

Getting back to the conservatory, where Ally, buttoned up to the throat, is watering the ferns, we see that between the conservatory and the garden, there is a passion-fruit vine. White stars, etched in purple and green, these are the passion flowers. And there are passion-fruit. Purple eggs of passion-fruit. They hang between the cool wet comfort of the conservatory and the murmuring haze of the garden where the bees are in the lavender. Their wings are glassy, and they carry the messages from the dark. The bees carry the messages from the underworld, the secret Celtic wisdom which is held deep in Daphne's heart.

Daphne is in the garden with the bees. With the lavender and with the bees. The aunts hope that she will not be stung. So many bees. At this time of year. Daphne is five. She is the daughter of the niece of the aunts. She is in the garden with the bees, and she has round pink cheeks, fat legs, a brown velvet dress, white pinny with windmills embroidered on it, and lace-up brown shoes. What a relief that the family failing of crippled feet has not been passed on to Daphne.

The world is feet. Daphne is five, and the world is feet. Little black boots, shiny boots, in the world of feet. Skirts swish and sway across the top of the boots. These aunts wear swoopy, swishy skirts of dark, dark, dark. The skirts are dark and secret and they smell. They smell of dust and boots and a little bit of piss. And lavender. There is some lavender in the smell of the aunts.

Out in the garden, there is lavender. And there is a pomegranate tree. On the tree, there are big globes of golden scarlet fruit. The skin of the fruit splits open. There are the seeds. Crimson seeds in shiny rows of crimson jelly. Juicy, juicy. The juice is clean and sweet. Crimson. There is crimson-purple on the edges of the seeds. The seeds shine with pomegranate. Daphne is eating the pomegranates.

Where are Daphne's mother and father? Well, they have had a baby, and they have brought Daphne here to stay with the aunts while the disturbance of having a baby settles down. Gosh. So Daphne is staying here with the surgical boots and the glass eye and the burgundy beret while the whole universe changes and her mother and father produce the new baby. Today is Sunday, day of roast dinners, and the baby is being brought to stay with the aunts while the mother and father go off to Mass. So Daphne, who is pushing her face into a pomegranate, juice running down her chin onto her pinny, is really waiting for her mother and father who will soon arrive with her baby sister. The baby sister is called Violet. Baby Violet is coming soon.

Yes, here are Daphne's mother and father and baby Violet. Mother is pretty, with a blue linen coat and a white hat. There are primroses, silk primroses, on her lapel. And Father is in his brown suit, with his yellow tie. He is all polished, and smelling of soap. His hair is spikey. They come up the path, the gravel path. The gravel path is edged with pink bricks. And there are bees and lavender. In a big wicker pram, under a mound of white satin and lace, is baby Violet. She is still and pink and good. She is a quiet baby. Baby Violet.

Daphne has pomegranate juice on her pinny. Her pinny with the windmills is stained with the crimson-purple of the pomegranates. She has been eating pomegranates again.

Baby Violet, in her pram, is put in the conservatory. It is so cool and quiet and shady and ferny and pitter patter . . . in the conservatory. Mother and Father are going out to Mass. Baby Violet and Daphne, and Ally, and Sissy, and Mags will stay here. They will stay here until Mother and Father come home from Mass, and then there will be the Sunday roast—wing rib, tomato pie, mint peas, cauliflower cheese. Mags is in the kitchen, cooking the cauliflower cheese.

Mags is in the kitchen cooking the cauliflower cheese. She is wearing her burgundy beret. Sissy is in the parlour, polishing the piano. She is wearing her teeny weeny glass eye. Ally is in the conservatory, watering the ferns. She is in her long dark skirt. Ally, Sissy, and Mags are all wearing their surgical boots. Clop, stump they go about their business.

Daphne is standing under the passion-fruit vine. Mother and Father have gone to Mass. They will be back for the Sunday roast. Baby Violet is in her yellow wicker pram in the conservatory with the ferns.

Ally puts down the watering can. She pats her skirt. Then she turns on the heel of her boot and goes out the door. Ally goes through the doorway, under the passion-fruit vine, and down the side path to the lavatory. Ally is going to the lavatory. She shuts herself into the tiny cubby house. It is decorated with morning glory. The top of the green door is serrated. There is a big iron handle on the door.

Daphne is standing under the passion-fruit vine, covered in pomegranate. She looks at the pram. She tiptoes over to the pram. Outside, the bees are buzzing. Aunt Ally is going to the lavatory. Baby Violet is asleep. She is pretty. She is round and fat and pretty. Violet is wearing a white frilly bonnet. Her eyelashes are soft and sweet and golden on her cheeks. Daphne puts one pointy finger on Violet's round pink cheek. Violet hums. She stirs. She hums again. Daphne pulls back the pram cover. She sees the baby's hands. They are nearly transparent. Little pink fingernails. Slowly, softly, quietly, Daphne peels back the covers. There is Violet. She is a baby in a dress. She has booties and a bonnet and a fine white bib. Baby Violet.

Being very careful, Daphne pulls Violet from the pram. She is holding her. She is standing very still and she is holding the baby. In the conservatory, there are ferns and cool and damp and Daphne is holding the baby. The baby hums. Daphne tiptoes round the conservatory. She is a very naughty girl.

"Put that baby down, you naughty girl!"

Ally, named after the beautiful Queen Alexandra, is clomping and stumping down the path, gravel rolling under her footsteps.

"Put that baby down at once!"

Daphne is frightened. Her hands let go. With what seems like no noise, the bundle of dress and bootie and bonnet and baby falls to the floor. It is the floor of the conservatory. The floor of the conservatory is black and white. It is black and white marble. The baby is lying on the floor of the conservatory, and she is crying. Baby Violet is screaming. Well, at least she is alive.

Everyone is suddenly there. Mags grabs the baby. Ally grabs Daphne. Sissy is wringing her polishing cloth in her hands. Scream, scream baby. The baby is screaming.

The floor is marble. She has dropped the baby on a marble floor. The baby will die. The baby will be an idiot. The baby will have a broken spine, a cracked skull. The baby will be a cripple.

The world is little black boots, little flying black laced boots.

Daphne has been beaten around the legs with a walking stick. Violet is back in her pram. She continues to cry. Daphne is shut in a cupboard under the stairs until her mother and father come back. They come back; she is released; the story is told; the baby is fed and pacified. Everybody goes to the dining room for the roast dinner which Mags has been so busy preparing all this time. Nobody has the heart to play the piano.

Now we drift into the past tense again.

After dinner, Mother and Father took the children home— Daphne and baby Violet. Mags in her beret went back to the kitchen to wash the dishes. Sissy and Ally went for a little walk in the garden. So there were the three sisters, in their boots, together in their home, after the terrible excitement of the day. What would become of the baby, they wondered. What would become of the awful Daphne?

It was getting dark. The bees had gone. The two sisters in the garden passed under the passion-fruit vine, went through the conservatory, and into the dark house. All the dishes were done, and the house was quiet. The three ladies sat down in the parlour with their knitting.

You will be wondering whether Violet was damaged by the fall. The only effect we know of was that she grew up to be very fond of ferns. But that may have been coincidental.

Ally, and her two sisters, died. We can suppose that they were buried with their boots. Certainly the glass eye. Perhaps even the beret. The passion-fruit vine (it was a Nelly Kelly) went wild.

And bees, descendants of those very glassy bees who witnessed the dropping of the baby on the marble floor, still hover over the lavender. Humming.

One with the Lot

I had a pink cotton cardigan I used to wear with a linen dress. I was fourteen. The cardigan had glass buttons shaped like stars that came off a card of Lovely Lady Buttons with a picture of Ida Lupino. My mother knitted the cardigan; she was always knitting. I sewed on the buttons carefully. There were six of them and the second from the top was out of line. I never used to do them up. "Do up your cardigan," my mother would say and I would start to do it up but when I got around the corner out of her sight I would undo it and let it flop back, flop away so that you could see the shape of nice little breasts under my linen dress. The dress was floral. It had a white background and blades of grass in clumps and bunches of primroses, and tulips that reminded me of little pink mouths. So it was really yellow and pink and green and white with a white linen collar on which my mother had sewn rick-rack braid, some green, some yellow and some pink. It was all meant to be sweet and innocent and it probably was if you did up your cardigan. And under the dress I had a white nylon petticoat my father gave me with a frill embroidered in red silk. They were hearts, red silk hearts, and they were on the pants as well. The bra I wore was a Maidenform with a sharp point over each nipple and circles and circles of little stitches like on a breastplate. It was the points that stuck through the linen dress and you could see them if you didn't do up the cardigan. Advertisements for Maidenform used to have a picture of a girl in a bra. The girl would be in some very unusual or inappropriate setting. So she would look like for instance the lady from the Unicorn Tapestries except her bra would be visible and it would say under the picture, "I dreamed I was a medieval maiden in my Maidenform bra". The one I liked best was the one that said, "I dreamed I took the bull by the horns," but you didn't see that one very often.

There was also white linen with the rick-rack on the pockets of the dress. Because it was hot I was wearing white sandals and no stockings. My legs were white and very smooth because I had just shaved them with a little green Milady razor and I had also sandpapered them with a Silkymit. Under my arms I just did with the razor, and I had plucked my eyebrows. I knew a girl who used to pluck the hairs on her arms. My lipstick was pale pink to match the cardigan and very thick. There was a place in George Street called the Rainbow where girls from school were not allowed to go. It was out of bounds because you met boys there and had ice-cream sundaes and it smelt of sour milk and Californian Poppy Oil. I was meeting Geoffrey Reynolds in the Rainbow and we had enough money between us to have the special which was One with the Lot. My linen dress had a full circle skirt that my mother had gone to a lot of trouble over. Geoffrey was sixteen. Once I made it up in my diary that he kissed me and my mother read it and I wasn't supposed to see him. It seemed pointless to explain I was making the diary up; not only pointless but embarrassing, and probably worse. There was a person I had really kissed the time I wrote it up as Geoffrey. This was Harvey Chappell and he was brainy and couldn't dance and only said about three things all night. Once he said he was reading a book about people who were so poor they had to eat baby crocodiles. I think it was in New Guinea or somewhere. Harvey's mother had the most awful way of cutting up oranges. She would get the orange on the vegetable board and cut it in half, like through the equator. Then she would put the halves cut-side down on the board and cut really thin slices. Then she scraped the board into the sink and put the slices on a pink saucer. She would sit down at the

kitchen table and pull the flesh of the orange off the slices with her
teeth. She had very terrible false teeth. And she would wipe her
mouth with her apron and tip the slices of orange peel into a sheet
of newspaper to wrap up for the garbage. Bits of orange stayed
stuck in her teeth. Harvey was nice really but he trod on my foot.
So I met Geoffrey in the Rainbow and we ordered spiders as well as
One with the Lot which meant two kinds of ice-cream and straw-
berry syrup and fruit and cream and nuts and chocolate shavings
and a glacé cherry and wafers and two spoons in a huge glass dish
like a boat. I was wearing vanilla as perfume and my Eastern Star
ring. Geoffrey and I were sitting tight up against each other in the
corner where people in the street couldn't see us. I took off my cardigan because I was hot and got syrup down the front of my dress
just a little bit. I was thinking about what I wrote in the diary and
wishing it was true and wondering how it would be if I said anything
about it as a sort of joke somehow. Then he put his arm right around
me and I felt really quite uncomfortable and wanted to run. The
table had a grey and white marble top. I just kept slowly digging my
spoon into the ice-cream and nuts and syrup and pushing it against
the side of the dish and then eating. It would melt in my mouth and
slide down easily but the taste was very sickly and I had to chew the
nuts. For some reason it was embarrassing sitting there with
Geoffrey's arm around me, saying nothing, and chewing and swal-
lowing. I had eaten off my lipstick by then. The main reason the
Rainbow was out of bounds was because you would kiss and cuddle
in there and later on there would be passionate scenes in parked
cars and on verandas. The sort of scene I would never actually put
in my diary whether I was making it up or not. This was the first
time I had ever been to the Rainbow and Geoffrey was kissing my
hair and so I swallowed a big blob of ice-cream and turned around
so we could kiss on the lips. And we did. It was completely different
from Harvey because Geoffrey kind of pushed his tongue between
my teeth and I was surprised at first but I liked it slipping in and out
like a lizard. Afterwards we didn't finish the sundae and I left my
cardigan on the seat. I meant to go back for it but I never did.

Goczka

He was red, dressed in red, and his horse was red.

My eye is looking out through the blanket. If I keep very still and stay under the blanket, I will be warm and safe, safe and warm. Still and safe and warm. I am the little boy under the grey blanket, scratchy blanket, warm and safe and scratchy. I am four now and I am under the blanket with just my eye peeping. I peep. My eye is peeping and I peep. Still, still, I am still. I am Goczka and I am very, very still. I wear the blanket like a hood, safe hood. The hood will save me from the night and the dark and the wolf. Rocked in the soft, soft swaying pink waters, womb waters, pink waters, I am the baby, safe baby, warm baby, soft baby. Wrapped in the waters, I rock and I sing, I am Goczka. The blanket, grey blanket is scratchy and safe. It is the pink waters, silk waters, my darling, my mother, my cradle, my pod. I am curled in my pod in the silver pink garden. I am curled in my pod in the garden. I peep from my pod. My eye is peeping, pod peeping. There is a smell of mould. There is a war. I peep from my blanket and I see that there is a war.

He was red, dressed in red, and his horse was red.

In Poland, there is a war. I am four years old, and here is the war. The children will be safe. Safe warm children in scratchy blankets, grey blankets, war blankets. The children are peeping from their blankets. Fifty children peeping from their blankets. Fifty children peeping from their blankets. Fifty children peeping from their blankets. There is a smell of war, a smell of blankets, a smell of mould. I do not know these children, I do not know this place. I am four, I am sad. I am crying in the war. They have put us in a church. We will be safe in the church. The walls are stone, old stone, cold stone. We are safe in the church in the war.

I do not know these children. They are babies, they are crying. The children are crying. I want my sister. My sister in her skirt, red skirt, thick skirt, thick red skirt. There is a silver ribbon in her hair. The ribbons on her skirt are dancing in the sunlight. My sister is dancing in the sunlight. She is Yadi, sister Yadi, and she holds me and she loves me and she is my sister. Sister Yadi. I am peeping from my blanket. I am looking for my sister. I am Goczka, she is Yadi, and I cry.

With my peeping eye, I see a window. Picture window. It is glass, it is sunset, it is sunshine in the sunset. Sweet sweetie shapes of lolly glass. I see the lolly glass and I am peeping at the glass. Glass. I see the glass, glassy glass. Red glass, blood glass. Sweet glass, sweetie glass, jar of lollies, lolly glass. Yadi gives me lollies is my sister is my lollies glassy lollies sugar lollies in the glass.

We are having cabbage soup. Sit up now and drink this cabbage soup there is a war. Spilling soup slop soup yellow wee wee soup the smell of old old socks mould old socks. And incense. In the church there lurks the old incense. It is hanging in the corners, in the dust of all the corners. There is incense in the corners of the church.

When I was a little boy, little Goczka, little boy, I was sitting with my sister by the fire. Goczka, little Goczka, listen Goczka, to the stories I will tell.

This is the story, she said, of Baba Yaga. Near the house was a dense forest; in the forest was a clearing, in the clearing there was a hut; and in this hut lived Baba Yaga. She let no one near her and devoured children as if they were chickens. The trees creaked. The dry leaves crackled. And she devoured children. The door opened and Baba Yaga went in whistling and whirling. The fence around the hut was made of human bones.

Fear not. Eat and pray, and go to sleep. Night will bring help.

Goczka is lying in the church in Poland in the war and it is getting dark. He can see the stained glass window if he peers from his blanket. In the sunset, the window glows with crimson fire. It is Saint George. They tell me I am George, I am Goczka, I am George. He is killing his dragon, red dragon. Killing his dragon. There are stones. In the picture in the window, there are stones. A long thin spear, a wide red cloak, and the stones. It is bright, it is light and Goczka is killing his dragon. I am Goczka. I kill.

He was red, dressed in red, and his horse was red.

In the church with all the children, there is a woman. She looks after us. She brings us the blankets, the soup, the bread, the day and the night. Eat, pray, and go to sleep. Night will bring help. In the morning, the war will be over. It will all be over, won't it?

You have to go to sleep now. Sleep now. No more crying, no more running down the church. If you are good and go to sleep, the war will get over, and we can all go home. Be good, and go to sleep. The woman says go to sleep. I will tell you a story, she says. She says there will be a story. Once upon a time, there was a witch and this witch was called Baba Yaga.

She is telling us the story Yadi told. Yadi, sister Yadi, lovely Yadi.

And she devoured little children as if they were chickens. And if you do not go to sleep, if you do not go to sleep, the door will fly open, and Baba Yaga will come whistling and whirling down the church in her great big black cloak, and she will eat you and crunch you and spit out the bones. If you don't go to sleep. Keep quiet and go to sleep. It is the war. She said she is the teacher. She said she is the grandmother. Grandmother soup, grandmother bread, soup and bread and Baba. My Baba makes lace. She is a lady making lace. She sits in the sunshine making lace. Flicking flying bobbins pins and bobbins making lace. My Baba smells of sugar making Sunshine lace. She sometimes smells of custard and vanilla. My vanilla Baba. She sings a lullaby, lace lullaby—sleep, little baby, the red bee hums. Sloneczko, hums, the red bee hums. Sleep, sleep sloneczko, my baby, my bee.

The woman is the teacher, cabbage teacher. She is the Baba of the war. Black Baba. Big black wolfy wolfy Baba. Pull up the blanket, Goczka. It is not safe to stay awake. It is not safe to go to sleep. It is not safe. It is the war.

You will be safe in the church, with the Baba, with the children, with the blankets, with the windows. There is incense in the corner. And if you do not go to sleep, Baba Yaga will get you.

So I lie in my blanket and it is getting dark. I watch the window. The night will bring help, the window will bring help. I love the window. The window is going to save me. Lovely window loves me. All around me, I smell crying. The children are crying in the church, safe church, in the war. It is dark. If you do not go to sleep, the doors will open and she will come, Baba Yaga will get you.

Saint George is killing the dragon. There is incense in the corners. The floor is stone. There is a wind outside. Outside there is a wind, a war and a wind. Stones and the dark and a war and a great big wind. And a whirling and whistling and a war.

I am getting cold.

He was red, dressed in red, and his horse was red.

There is still and quiet here now. We are all listening to the wind, the wind outside. The window is all dark now. Dark like snow. Some of the children have fallen asleep. Once upon a time, there were some children and they got into a boat and fell asleep. They fell asleep in the boat. It was a dark boat, the children's boat. The trees beside the water met across the water. And the children fell asleep in the boat. They floated down the river, dark, sweet river. They floated down the river in the boat.

The window is black.

I am four years old and I am Goczka and there is always a war. My sister is Yadi, and she has gone, gone with the war. Her skirt is red, her red skirt, and it is gone with her silver ribbons in the war. I am rocking in the red skirt, in the grey blanket, in the dark. There is a rustle. I hear a rustle. The leaves are crackling. The door is creaking. It is creaking cracking open. The night is coming in. Into the church, the night is coming. Night will bring help.

If you do not go to sleep, Baba Yaga, the Baba Yaga will come and get you. I will go to sleep, I will go to sleep. I am going to sleep by the window. I am peeping and I am going to sleep.

Very high, very wide, very black, very full, into the cavern of the church where the fifty children are lying, the Baba Yaga comes. If you are asleep, you will not see her. If you are awake, she will get you. She is here. She is flapping slowly down the church. Moaning and howling, she is coming to get the children. Wild wisps of witch's hair wild wisps of hair. She is black, she is scratched, she will get you. If you do not go to sleep she will get you.

Goczka, little Goczka, close your eye, no more peeping. The Baba Yaga is here. She smells of cabbage soup. She is here with her claws. She is here.

The blanket is not safe.

There is a war. Goczka, sloneczko, there is a war.

She said she is the grandmother. She is wearing a big black cloak, wolfy cloak.

I melt into the blanket. I melt into the window. I am killing the dragon. Goczka is big, he is big inside. He is strong to kill the dragon, the dragon in the window. Quiet now, still, still. Safe in Goczka's heart, he is safe in his heart. In his heart, in my heart, there is a giant giant window. It is red and red and red. There is war, there is the Baba, there is whirling creaking crackling. All is whistling. She is flapping and whirling.

I will not go to sleep. I will not sleep. I am big and bright and strong.

I am red, dressed in red, and my horse is red.

Cave Amantem

The girl is burying the body in the hollow. She has wrapped it in a scarlet cloak. In the hollow beneath the sweet pines, she is burying the body which she has wrapped in the cloak. She scatters sweet herbs across the dead one who is folded and parcelled in scarlet. The girl scatters herbs and wild flowers, pine needles, pebbles. There is a patter of pebbles; there is a rustle of leaves.

Tears. There are tears in her eyes, on her fingers, lightly falling sometimes, upon the brush of greenery veiling the body in its cloth. Her pale eyes are filled with tears. Tears glisten on the leaves. In the hollow, the girl is burying the body, as her tears slide down the leaves, beading the green. Tears, rolling across rocks, shiver and settle between pebbles. They make no stain on the scarlet cloth, for the cloth is grimy, tattered at the edges, toggled with mud. It shows through the leaves and flowers, now dull red, now brown, and sometimes, on the edge of a wrinkle, vivid blood. Somewhere, the girl has gathered twigs of rosemary. She sprinkles the leaves of her rosemary across the body in the hollow.

In the hollow between the rocks, beneath the sweet pines, in the heart of the silence of the forest, the girl is burying the body. Her fingernails, like claws, damaged, stained, scratch at the earth which she drops, crumbles, on top of the garlands of greenery. Stones, small rocks, and crumbs of earth. Moist and rotting leaves.

It has taken her all day. In the castle, whole save for the roof, she wrapped the body in her cloak and carried it and dragged it to the hollow. She placed it on the rotting floor of the sweet pine forest, and covered it with leaves and earth. Her arms were strong; she carried rocks; she marked the place with rocks. She wept when she buried the body of the wolf.

Isabella had a terrible reputation. She used to go up to the old castle—there is no roof—with just about anyone. Soldiers, musicians, cripples, foreigners, old men, and boys. She was reasonably pretty, in a sly sort of way. Oh, but there was the devil in her eyes. Light eyes, too light for hereabouts. Black hair, light eyes—Isabella was always a strange one. Pretty enough, you know, but strange.

Well, none of the decent young men of the village would have very much to do with her. Everybody thought she would never find a husband. But she didn't care very much about that. She lived with her grandmother, and she knew she would inherit the house when the old lady died. Inherit the house and the pigs and the hens and the few poor olive trees and the little herb garden. The old lady sold herbs. And she was so good and respectable and proud. There she was at Mass every day of her life; on feast days she wore a mantilla given to her long ago by the old Count. That is, the father of the present Count. She kept her house as clean as a convent with white walls and bright blue doors—even on the cupboards. I used to go there often—the chairs were made from bent withies; the table was blue. I would collect the eggs and stop for a gossip. Lace, there was lace, pure white. The grandmother made lace. Oh, she was an industrious old woman. And pious. There she was at Mass, as I said, every morning, with her beads and her proud eyes and her prayers.

She prayed, that old woman, for a husband for Isabella. What a joke! But she did. And she prayed as she swept the flagstones of her parlour, as she scrubbed the wooden staircase. She was making a wedding dress for Isabella, you know. Linen and lace and the sheets and all the household linens. She made the dress for my daughter Caterina when she married the Count's nephew. She was known for miles around for her beautiful wedding gowns. But she couldn't do a thing with Isabella.

Nobody could do anything with Isabella. She always went her own way. The nuns did their best to tame her, and then they just gave up and prayed for her. The candles that have been lit for that girl! The old grandmother was far too weak. What Isabella needed, I say, was a father and half a dozen brothers to straighten her out.

And that red cloak—she always wore that cloak. You could see her coming for miles. Of course, her grandmother made it for her. It would have been fine for a princess on a white horse. But there it was on Isabella as she ran from one end of the village to the other, often barefoot, meeting soldiers and travelling musicians and so on in the forest.

So the grandmother swept the floor and she prayed and she made lace pillow covers and she prayed and she prayed for a husband for her beautiful Isabella. Everyone felt very sorry for her, the poor old woman. While Isabella roamed round like a gipsy, just like a gipsy in her red velvet cloak. Her skin was white, you know, just touched with apricot. The grandmother was like an old walnut, and she seemed to be made from roots of trees. Yes, she looked like the roots of trees, the grandmother, the walnut. The granddaughter was the ripe fruit. Oh, she was a juicy apricot.

My son was half in love with her—half the time. He knew it was madness. He knew not to go near her. But he liked the idea of inheriting the poor little farm, and he did like the idea of going with Isabella. I warned him that if he did, I would beat him within an inch of his life. He laughed and said he would put me down the well—ah, but he knew that I meant what I said. And he knew that I was right, in the end.

He has since married the niece of a distant relative of the bishop, and stands to inherit a flock of sheep and a wide pastureland. But I don't mind telling you that he did plan to marry Isabella.

My son was the answer to the grandmother's prayers. Heaven

saw the candles she lit; the Mother of Sorrows heard the litanies she mumbled; and my son was to be, she thought, the answer to it all. He is very pleased now, naturally, that I stepped in. I knew what I was doing, as far as both families were concerned. They would have been no good for each other, Isabella and Luis. And our family has always been very respectable, with scarcely a breath of scandal, ever. My nephew is an idiot—but that is a different story. And for all that Isabella was a whore, she was really rather simple.

I went to her, that afternoon, and I said I had an errand for her. Well, she trusted me. I think now that perhaps she trusted everybody, and that was the funny thing about her. She wanted to please me, because I was the mother of Luis. I asked her to take a basket of cakes to my sister. Little sugared cakes—to my sister who lives on the other side of the forest. The great pine forest you see out there. She, that is, my sister, was giving a party for the nuns. So I packed a basket with the cakes—I am well known around here for my little sugared cakes—and the tiny glasses—so delicately cut—the ones that my sister always likes to use—I sometimes wish that she would get some of her own—and I called Isabella over, and I asked her to take the basket of things to my sister. I said she could be back by sundown—and indeed so she could, if she hurried. But Isabella was one to dawdle, you know. I knew that she had an arrangement to meet Luis at the old castle at sundown. He was there; she wasn't. I know that he must have heard the wolves, but he has never spoken of it.

They found my basket and the tiny glasses, so delicately cut, all of them broken, and some of the little sugared cakes, strewn across the forest floor. I have replaced the glasses. It was not so difficult.

I told them I had asked her to do the errand. Of course I told them. I will never be able to forgive myself. Everyone knew that I was only trying to be friendly, and to include her in some useful way in a family celebration. With Luis so besotted with her. The big fool. Yes, I admitted it was my basket—my best—my glasses, my cakes. My errand. My errand sent her to her doom in the forest. How can I ever forgive myself? Luis has forgiven me now. He is married, as

I said, to one of the relatives of the bishop. They will have a son in the spring.

No, they never found a trace of Isabella. Not even a piece of her grandmother's lace. Her grandmother waited. She waited for a year for that girl to come back. The old lady spoke to nobody but the priest. And then, one night, she died. Of grief. She died with quiet dignity, of grief. Oh, and old age, of course. She was a twisted tree root, and she died—of old age. And of grief.

She loved Isabella. She really loved Isabella. The wedding dress was on the bed, I believe. It was the finest lacework the nuns have ever seen. I have not seen it myself—but the nuns said it was the finest spiderweb of lace—and white—so white. Shiny. With tear-drops of crystal. A dress for the Madonna. So they put it on the statue in the convent. It seemed the only thing to do.

They never found Isabella's body. If they had found it, they would have buried her in the dress. Naturally. But Isabella was never found. The men went out searching through the forest, every night, every day for months. It became an obsession with them. Whenever a stranger appeared in the village, they would tell him the story of Isabella, and get up a hunting party to go out after the wolves. But in all the two years since it happened, they never got one. Until two nights ago.

Two nights ago, some soldiers from the north said they injured a wolf, the leader. The Devil with the fires of Hell in his eyes, they said. Well, maybe they got the animal. But Isabella, they never found.

I had a long talk to the priest about my part in the tragedy. He said that I was not to know, and that I must never dwell on the idea that I sent the girl into the forest to her doom. She went, after all, of her own free will. I was not to know. But what a fate, what a pun-ishment! To be eaten by wolves. It's the grandmother I feel most sorry for. Because, you know, she never really knew who that girl was. Her son brought the baby home from France. Said she was his daughter, and that the mother had died. Then he—a soldier he was—died of a fever, and the grandmother brought the girl up. She did her best, but I knew it would never work out. Everybody knew that it would never work out. And it didn't. Not a trace they found of her. Not a trace. Nothing.

The girl in the tattered lace dress is burying the body. Toggled with mud, the cloak parcels the dead. In the sweet pine forest, the girl has wrapped the wolf in her scarlet cloak. With tears and ceremony, herbs and stones, she is burying him in the hollow. She is silent. There is a bitter smell; there is a sweet smell; he is dead.

She is burying him in the forest.

Every Home Should Have a Cedar Chest

Lay up for yourself treasure in heaven, where neither moth nor rust doth corrupt.

The larvae of the cosmopolitan clothes moth attack wool, hair, silk, carpets, feathers, furs, and dried skins.

Clothing and fur insurance are what you buy when you invest in a cedar chest—a safe, moth-proof storage space, beautiful as well as practical. The moths that you see flying around do no damage; it is the young moth worms, deposited as eggs in dark and concealed places that destroy clothing. The United States Government Department of Agriculture has definitely ascertained that cedar chests have a pronounced killing effect on moth worms. It is recommended that in using a cedar chest for the protection of clothing, fabric, and furs, special care should be taken to prevent undue escape of the aroma. The chests should remain tightly closed as much as possible.

Every home should have a cedar chest.

Furnish your home with one of these splendid cedar chests.

149

A chest that breathes of romance, with its suggestion of pirates' treasure trove. Made of genuine red cedar from the forests of California, furnished in natural cedar colour, with a coating of genuine Duco. Neatly ornamented with two-inch copper bands, studded with round copper head nails. Easy rolling casters. Equipped with substantial lock and key.

Puerto Rican hand embroidered costume slips possess a distinctive individuality. Fine enough for the most fastidious woman and lovely enough for the daintiest trousseau this step-in slip of silk crepe-de-chine is topped with dainty and fine quality lace and insertion, and is finished with lace edging. The embroidered net medallion and the lace insertion and the clusters of pintucks add an elaborate touch.

Peach, white, black, purple.

For the trim figure in fashion's favour, you will want these lovely high grade rayon and silk jersey knit bloomers. They have the clinging softness of real silk, yet are made full and roomy. Have reinforced double fabric gusset crotch, elastic waist and pretty lace-edged ruffle at elastic knees. Launder beautifully in soap suds.

Here you will find comfortable, scientifically designed brassieres for practically every type of figure. Brassieres should conform to the natural outlines of the figure—their chief purpose is to hold flesh immovable, not to compress it into much smaller space than it naturally occupies. The too tight brassiere affords one of the quickest possible means of spoiling the lines of the figure. Do not spoil, but improve or preserve those youthful lines. It will be to your advantage to follow our instructions "How to measure": Straighten back and shoulders; place tape measure around body under arms, pull smoothly, not too tight over fullest part of bust and give actual measurement in inches. If your bust measurement is thirty-five inches, order size thirty-six; all brassieres are made in even sizes only.

Peach, white, flesh, orchid.

This long brassiere is specially designed for stylish trim figure lines. Made of firm cotton with fancy silk elastic insets in the sides. Special stay-flat boning in front effectively controls the diaphragm.

Peach, white, flesh, orchid, rose.

Goats belong to the family of hollow-horned ruminants and are of the genus Capra, closely allied to the sheep. The goat has long been used as a source of milk, cheese, mohair, and meat, and its skin has been valued as a source of leather.

Europe's best offering of fine quality kid gloves made of real kid skins with the popular petit-point embroidered turnover cuffs. Handsomely embroidered backs.

Black, grey, beaver, champagne.

Match your gloves with our special dog and wolf fur collar and cuff sets.

The eastern red cedar of America is much used in cabinet-making. With its suggestion of pirates' treasure trove.

Lay up for yourself treasure in heaven.

To be smartly dressed, you must be correctly corseted. Stylehint: Shape your figure into slim lines of beauty by wearing the lovely Pliant-B.

The baleen whales are distinguished from others by the possession of a double series of triangular horny plates anchored to the roof of the mouth. The inner side of these is frayed out into a fringe of bristles. The fringes combine to form a matted sieve or strainer for collecting the planktonic animals on which baleen whales depend for nourishment. It is these bristles, known as whalebone, which are used in corsets.

Shape your figure into slim lines of beauty by wearing lovely Pliant-B.

Lower part in front and at sides of back is shaped like a girdle and is cleverly fashioned of various sections of one-piece elastic. It hugs the body ever so comfortably, thereby subtly bringing out the feminine line. Fastens with a broad-end clasp at direct body centre. The front panel of fine rayon fabric cares for the bust and fits neatly over the lower part, giving a flat front and longer figure lines. The elastic along the entire bottom edge cups the figure snugly, giving trim hip lines, and it expands comfortably when seated. Moderately boned with genuine whalebone. Six large suspenders. Creates a stylish contour, supports the abdomen in its proper position, reduces the hips and abdominal girth, and does away with the pushing of flesh into unsightly bulges, and the compression of the diaphragm. Can be laundered freely without injury. Lacing at sides and bottom front permits wonderful adjustment. Bends with the body.

Available in: peach, white, flesh.

The common silkworm is native to China. The food of its caterpillars is the leaves of the mulberry tree. The silk produced in the cocoons is of the highest quality, and highly sought-after.

Natural, brown, platinum grey.

And for a very effective appearance on the garment, add one of our squirrel belly fur trims.

Beige-tan, mink-brown, platinum-grey.

The larvae of the cosmopolitan clothes moth attack wool, hair, silk, carpets, feathers, furs, and dried skins.

The wood of the cedar is decay-resistant and insect-repellant. Every home should have a cedar chest.

Cedar is the name applied to a variety of trees, both gymnosperms and angiosperms, most of which are evergreen and have aromatic, often red-tinged wood which in many cases is decay-resistant and insect-repellant. Several species have fine, durable wood used for timber and for cigar boxes, chests, and closets. The eastern red cedar of America is much used in cabinet-making, for posts, and in the manufacture of pencils.

Every home should have a cedar chest.

Made of genuine red cedar, mostly ornamented with two-inch copper bands, studded with round copper head nails, easy rolling casters, lined with satin, decorated with crucifix or plain cross. It hugs the body ever so comfortably. Clusters of pintucks add an elaborate touch. The clinging softness of real silk.

Lay up for yourself treasure in heaven, where neither moth nor rust doth corrupt.

Pirate's treasure trove.

Peach, white, flesh, Nile green.